W9-BNW-678

Praise for Linda Winstead Jones

"*Raintree: Haunted,* by Linda Winstead Jones, is nonstop action from start to finish. Jones' characters are compelling, and her story is both exciting and original. Readers won't want to put it down!"
—*RT Book Reviews*

Praise for Lisa Childs

"When Damien Gray comes into contact with the ghost of his wife…he realizes she's dead and trying to communicate with him. In Childs's gripping tale, Damien's grief and Olivia's anger are convincingly depicted, and there are some surprising twists."
—*RT Book Reviews* on *Immortal Bride*

Praise for Bonnie Vanak

"Wolf shapeshifter Damian Marcel races against time to save Jamie Walsh, the woman destined to be his mate, from a curse that is slowly turning her to stone…. Bonnie Vanak's *Enemy Lover* offers nonstop excitement and great sexual tension."
—*RT Book Reviews*

LINDA WINSTEAD JONES

has written more than fifty romance books in several subgenres. She's won the Colorado Romance Writers Award of Excellence twice, is a three-time RITA® Award finalist and, writing as Linda Fallon, is the winner of the 2004 RITA® Award for paranormal romance. Linda lives in northern Alabama with her husband of thirty-four years. Visit her Web site at www.lindawinsteadjones.com.

LISA CHILDS

has been writing since she could first form sentences. A Halloween birthday predestined a life of writing for the Nocturne line. She enjoys the mix of suspense and romance. Readers can write to Lisa at P.O. Box 139, Marne, MI 49435 or visit her at her Web site, www.lisachilds.com.

BONNIE VANAK

fell in love with romance novels during childhood. After years of newspaper reporting, Bonnie joined an international charity and tours destitute countries to write about issues affecting the poor. She turned to writing romance novels as a diversion from her job's emotional strain. Bonnie lives in Florida with her husband and two dogs. Visit her Web site at www.bonnievanak.com or e-mail her at bonnievanak@aol.com.

HOLIDAY WITH A
VAMPIRE III

LINDA WINSTEAD JONES
LISA CHILDS
BONNIE VANAK

Silhouette® Books

nocturne™

If you purchased this book without a cover you should be aware
that this book is stolen property. It was reported as "unsold and
destroyed" to the publisher, and neither the author nor the
publisher has received any payment for this "stripped book."

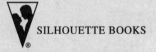

SILHOUETTE BOOKS

Recycling programs
for this product may
not exist in your area.

ISBN-13: 978-0-373-61824-8

HOLIDAY WITH A VAMPIRE III

Copyright © 2009 by Harlequin Books S.A.

The publisher acknowledges the copyright holders
of the individual works as follows:

SUNDOWN
Copyright © 2009 by Linda Winstead Jones

NOTHING SAYS CHRISTMAS LIKE A VAMPIRE
Copyright © 2009 by Lisa Childs-Theeuwes

UNWRAPPED
Copyright © 2009 by Bonnie Vanak

All rights reserved. Except for use in any review, the reproduction
or utilization of this work in whole or in part in any form by any
electronic, mechanical or other means, now known or hereafter
invented, including xerography, photocopying and recording, or in
any information storage or retrieval system, is forbidden without
the written permission of the editorial office, Silhouette Books,
233 Broadway, New York, NY 10279 U.S.A.

This is a work of fiction. Names, characters, places and incidents are
either the product of the author's imagination or are used fictitiously, and
any resemblance to actual persons, living or dead, business establishments,
events or locales is entirely coincidental.

This edition published by arrangement with Harlequin Books S.A.

® and TM are trademarks of Harlequin Books S.A., used under license.
Trademarks indicated with ® are registered in the United States Patent
and Trademark Office, the Canadian Trade Marks Office and in other
countries.

www.silhouettenocturne.com

Printed in U.S.A.

CONTENTS

SUNDOWN
Linda Winstead Jones

Dear Reader,

"Sundown" is my first vampire story. I enjoyed writing it so much that I don't think it will be the last.

A long while back, I was having lunch with writer friends, and we were talking about books and business in general. Somehow the conversation got turned around to vampires. (At these meetings anything and everything is fair game.) I was telling them that I'd never written a vampire story and probably never would. Then, somehow, I started talking about what the story might be like if I ever did take that plunge.

And from then on, Abby and Leo were speaking to me. People often ask about where ideas come from, and it's usually difficult to describe. But this one is easy. "Sundown" came out of a casual conversation over iced tea and a BLT.

Abby and Leo live in a different world. Their world is darker than mine; the stakes are high. I hope you enjoy reading their story.

Best,

Linda

For Danniele Worsham and Marilyn Puett,
"Children" I never thought to have.
May your futures be bright!

Chapter 1

The underlying thrum of heartbeats. Tempting scents and primitive urges denied. It was a night like thousands—tens of thousands—of others.

Abby stood behind the long, polished bar of her place, wiping down a beer mug until it shone like the row of gleaming glasses lined up behind her. She studied the customers, subtly keeping an eye on them much in the way a mother hen might, though no one who knew her well would mistake her for such a caring creature. On the other side of the room a number of round tables arranged around a small dance floor were populated by a mixture of vampires and humans, regulars for the most part. Things were quiet tonight, as Tuesdays often were. Friday and Saturday would be another story; weekends around here were rarely what anyone would call quiet.

The vampires here were, of course, acutely aware of the humans in their midst. Thirsty as they were, tempted as they might be by the scent of fresh blood and living flesh and the gentle, steady thudding of a dozen heartbeats beneath warm skin, they were not allowed to hunt within ten miles of Abby's place, and they were expressly forbidden to ever take the life of one of her customers. She was the oldest in town, and they respected—and even feared—the strength that came with centuries of survival in an unfriendly world. There was no official hierarchy, no appointed position. She was the strongest among those who gathered here, and so she led.

Abby did her best to show those of her kind who would listen that it wasn't necessary to take lives in order to survive. She wasn't tenderhearted and she didn't have any special fondness for humans, but logic drove her to be cautious and to convince others of the necessity. The existence of vampires was best served if there wasn't a constant stream of dead, bloodless humans to explain away. Besides, why kill when you could drink your fill, touch a weak mind and make your donor forget, and continue to live in one place for many years without fear of being discovered? Only the stupidest, the most out of control, killed their prey.

The humans who imbibed and talked and laughed in Abby's bar had no idea that they drank next to monsters, the stuff of fantastical nightmares. That was as it should be. Most of them lived in the neighborhood, mortals blind to the fact that some of the other customers in their favorite bar never actually drank the whiskey or beer placed before them. They didn't think it odd that the two groups never mingled, that there was an invisible but impenetrable wall between them. Instinct kept them from making friendly gestures toward the vampires; innate self-preservation prevented them from asking too many questions. They drank, sometimes too much. They paid, they laughed, they left the day's troubles behind. And they listened to Remy's music.

Remy played piano on the raised stage, his fingers moving with the ease brought on by more than two hundred years of practice. The piano itself was nothing special—it had been bought at a discount from a retiring piano teacher—but in Remy's hands the beat-up upright became special. Jazz was his favorite style, but in the hours the Sundown Bar was open to the public—to the living—he played to the crowd. Country and classic rock, for the most part, but always with a touch of the jazz he loved. No one played "Blue" quite like Remy, and he could bring the house down with "Sweet Home Alabama." At the moment Remy was using the surname Zeringue, but like Abby, he changed his last name often.

Abby had lived in a lot of different places over the years. Big cities, small towns and villages, mountain-top cabins, a cave—though not for very long—and an isolated farm or two. Budding Corner, Alabama, was a midsize town, large enough to keep her business profitable, small enough that the place wasn't overrun with rogue vamps, who usually preferred the anonymity and massive feeding ground of a large city. Here the air was clean, which was a comfort for her sensitive nose. The days were quiet and the residents were into easy living and minding their own business. What more could she ask for?

When the door to the windowless bar opened, almost every head in the room turned to see who was entering—no different from any other time that door swung in. Abby cursed beneath her breath, though the man who entered was a regular himself and she should be used to seeing him by now. Since Stryker had moved to Budding Corner a few short months back he'd stopped by her place almost every night, sometimes for a few minutes, other nights for hours. Abby wasn't bothered by cops. She paid her bills; she adhered to health codes and ABC regulations to the letter; she was very careful to do nothing that might call attention to her.

But this particular cop had been hanging around too often and too long. Detective Leo Stryker was observant—unlike the other humans in the room, unlike the large majority of the humans Abby met. There was something about him that made her nervous.

And he kept asking her out. On a date.

As Stryker approached the bar Abby grabbed a bottle of Jack Daniel's. Jack and Coke was his drink, and he never had more than one. Two on a really bad night a couple of months ago, but for the most part when his one drink was done and she turned down his always-charming offer of a date, he headed out the door. Leo left alone every time, even though more than one customer had made it clear that he didn't have to go home without a companion. He could get lucky in the parking lot night after night. But he didn't.

She placed a glass on the bar where Leo always sat, but he waved her off. "Nothing for me tonight," he said, taking his badge out and unnecessarily flashing it for her. "I'm here on official business."

Abby didn't allow her concern to show. Official business could be as simple as a patron parking their car where they should not, or a sign improperly displayed, or maybe one of her human customers was up to no good and he wanted to ask questions about that human. She smiled at him; he did not smile back as he usually did.

Leo took his usual bar stool and leaned onto the bar. If she was warm-blooded and into dating, she'd definitely accept his invitations. For a mortal he was quite handsome and well built, with medium-dark blond hair cut fairly short, but not severely so, expressive blue eyes and a strong jaw. His neck was thick and muscled and she could smell it from where she stood, a good four feet away. He had to be at least six foot two, a good twelve inches taller than she was, and he was a big guy—big arms, broad shoulders, large hands. Her mouth watered. It was the scent that got to her most strongly. She clenched her fists behind the bar, so he couldn't see her reaction. She was rarely so tempted, and it bothered her that this human had become something akin to a weakness.

It was past time for her to feed from a living, breathing human being with a heartbeat and deliciously warm skin, but she'd be an idiot to drink from an overly observant cop, no matter how tasty he smelled, no matter how pleasing he was to the eye. Besides, it wasn't as if she was about to break her own rules about tasting the customers.

"Do you know a girl by the name of Marisa Blackwell?"

"Sure," Abby said, momentarily relieved. What on earth could Marisa Blackwell have done to get herself into trouble? Marisa was a regular, a quiet, pretty young girl who seemed harmless enough. Still, looks could be deceiving. Abby herself was proof of that. "What did she do?"

Leo's expression hardened. "She got herself murdered, and her roommate says the Sundown Bar was her last stop."

Leo watched Abby for a reaction, as he always did when he questioned anyone concerning a murder. The news of Blackwell's death seemed to make Abby angry. She wasn't visibly shocked, she didn't cry or shake… but she was not unaffected.

"I'm so sorry," she said softly, her voice reaching inside him and grabbing, as it always did. "What happened?"

"It wasn't a natural death, I can tell you that much." He wasn't about to explain to her, or to anyone else, that the victim's blood had been drained from her body, that the pretty girl's throat had been practically torn out. He couldn't explain yet what had happened, but he didn't want to alarm anyone. If that tidbit hit the newspapers and the television news, there would be hell to pay. Budding Corner's only newspaper was a thin weekly filled with the escapades of the mayor and city councilmen, as well as a shitload of recipes and letters to the editor, and the closest television station was in Huntsville, so maybe he could keep the details quiet for a while. "Do you remember who she was with last night?"

Abby's eyes narrowed. Even though he was here on business tonight, he couldn't help but note—not for the first time—that she was a striking woman. Beautiful, yes, but the world was filled with beautiful women. This one was somehow different, and he'd known it from the first moment he'd laid eyes on her. Abby Brown had long, dark hair, pale green eyes, a body that wouldn't quit and a face that would've been at home on a statue of a goddess. Her plain, white, button-up shirt gaped when she moved just so, revealing a tiny little bit of swelling cleavage, but not so much that she was flashing the customers in order to get better tips. The sight was very nice, after a long, crappy day.

But what called him to her went beyond her looks. She was smart, she was savvy and she kept secrets. He knew it; he felt it in his bones; he saw it in her eyes. And dammit, he wanted to uncover every one of her secrets—along with what lay beneath that plain blouse and whatever else she wore. She was partial to longish skirts that offered no more than an occasional flash of calf, on the rare occasions she stepped out from behind the bar.

He kept asking her out and she kept turning him down. For many divorced men that rejection might be traumatic. Abby's refusals were never brutal, but there was a certainty in her eyes and in her voice that would've warned most men away. Far, far away. Leo intended to keep trying; he was known for his patience and persistence, and he wanted this woman. One of these days he'd wear her down. A woman like Abby would be worth a little trauma and a bruise or two to his ego.

"She came in with a friend of hers," Abby said, answering his question. "Alicia, I believe."

"Yes," Leo responded. "We spoke to Alicia this afternoon."

Abby stared a hole through him. "Then why did you ask me who she was with?"

"I'd like to know if Alicia remembers last night's events correctly."

Abby leaned into the bar, bringing her face closer to his—but not close enough to suit him. She breathed deeply, once. "Detective Stryker, be honest. You want to know if one of us would be so foolish as to lie to you."

He couldn't help but smile a little. "There is that. And how many times do I have to tell you to call me Leo? I've been in here damn near every night for the past three months." When he'd moved to this little podunk town and taken a job as an investigator with a department much smaller than the one in Birmingham, he'd taken a cut in pay and had traded his very nice condo for a ramshackle rental house at the edge of town, a house he kept telling himself was only temporary. It had been worth every sacrifice to get away from his ex and all the reminders of the years they'd spent together—good and bad. Finding a woman like Abby here had been a nice little bonus, or would be if she'd give him the time of day.

The woman he'd been fantasizing about for months had never stared at him quite this way. Her eyes met his and held them, and he could swear he felt that gaze to his soul. It burned a little, it invaded, and he couldn't help but squirm.

"The two girls came in together," she said, her voice smooth and sensual. "As they often do. They had margaritas, two each. They were approached by two men who are not regular customers, young men I would guess to be in their midtwenties, who brought them each another margarita. Around ten in the evening, Marisa left. Alone. Alicia left an hour or so later in the company of one of the gentlemen. The other stayed a while longer. I'm afraid I didn't get their names, and they paid cash."

That wasn't much more help than Alicia's story that the guys' names were Jason and Mike, no last names offered or asked for, and they were simply "traveling through." Alicia had taken Mike home with her, but where had Jason gone?

"Did you often see Marisa and her friends here so late on a work night?"

"Sometimes," she responded in a smooth voice.

"I don't suppose either of those men is here tonight." Leo turned on his bar stool to survey the room, knowing what her answer would be. He recognized everyone here.

"No," Abby said as Leo watched the cocktail waitress Margaret, a blonde who was almost as beautiful as her employer, serve a tray of bottled beers to an appreciative table. Every man there took a moment to study Margaret's nicely displayed cleavage or long legs, depending on their body part of interest. She didn't seem to be offended, but then, if you dressed that way it wouldn't make much sense to be easily offended by open appreciation.

"You seem to have a good memory," he said to the woman behind the bar. "Think you can provide a description for a sketch artist?"

"I can do better than that."

He spun around to face Abby once more. "How's that?"

She cocked her head slightly and it seemed that for a moment there was no one in the room but the two of them. Leo held his breath; he almost forgot why he was here.

"I'm a bit of an artist myself," Abby said. "After we close up tonight I'll draw the men as I remember them."

"Thanks." He leaned into the bar, wishing he could order a drink and stick around and just look at her for a while longer. She could certainly make a bad day better, if she put her mind to it. But tonight he had work to do. Marisa Blackwell's was the first murder in Budding Corner in seventeen years, and folks were excited. They were also worried. It hadn't been your normal robbery murder and it sure didn't look like your everyday domestic violence. Much as he wanted a drink, he wouldn't consider himself off duty until this case was solved. "Can I pick the sketches up in the morning?"

Abby smiled at him, but there was no warmth in her expression. The smile, like everything about her, was cool and controlled. Man, how he would love to make her lose control. How he wanted to discover the secrets beyond the cool exterior. "I'll stick them on the front door of the bar in the morning and you can pick them up at any time."

"I'd rather collect them from you, in case I have any more questions."

"That's not necessary, is it?"

He leaned over the bar. "I really don't like the idea of the sketches out in the open where anyone could snag them. It'll be best if I take them straight from your hand. Over lunch?"

Was that a smile? Maybe.

"If you must collect the sketches directly from me you can pick them up tomorrow night. We open at sundown, as you well know." She gestured to the red-and-gold neon sign behind her. The Sundown Bar. It was fine to have a gimmick, but wasn't this taking things too far? Her insistence in not opening until after sunset had made the summer days too long, and he was glad autumn had arrived and the nights were now a bit longer.

"We need those sketches as soon as possible. Is there any chance…"

Abby offered a hand over the bar, palm up. The fingers were long and pale and slender, and she wore no jewelry. No ring, no watch or bracelet. He was too old to be tempted this way, especially when he was working, but he had an almost uncontrollable urge to grab that hand and lick the palm. Just once.

"Do you have a card?" she asked, as he ignored the hand she offered. "I'll call you if I get the drawings finished sooner and wish to meet you earlier in the day."

"Sure." He fished a card out of his jacket pocket and laid it in her hand. The tips of his fingers brushed her palm, which seemed oddly cool. She'd been handling ice and cold bottles, he reminded himself as he stood, nodded and reluctantly headed for the door.

* * *

When the door had closed behind Leo, Abby dropped the card he'd given her in the trash can at her feet. She'd have to wait until 2:00 a.m., when the human customers would be forced to leave, and then she'd interrogate her vampire friends and patrons. Surely none of them would be so foolish as to not only feed upon but also kill one of her customers, but she'd plucked a vision from Leo's head and she knew Marisa had been attacked at her throat. A human might've attacked her there, but the wound he had remembered so vividly indicated a vampire, a vicious one—and if a vamp had done the deed it was likely he or she had been here. Like called to like, and besides, after two in the morning she served blood. This was the only place for two hundred miles or more that a vamp could order a pint. She served pigs' blood for the most part, which tasted like crap if it wasn't warmed properly. She had become an expert at preparing a safe, easy meal. Pigs' blood wouldn't entirely satisfy a vamp forever, but oftentimes it was enough.

Killing the customers was against Abby's rules, and though she was not the biggest or the physically strongest vampire in the world, or even in the country, she was the oldest and most powerful for hundreds of miles. At more than four hundred years old, she had powers those who flocked to her had not yet developed. The other vamps were drawn to her, they respected her; they obeyed her. Many newer vampires came here to learn from her, either sent by their makers or drawn by instincts they had not yet perfected and yet could not reject. She helped guide them to control, to hone whatever powers they'd been given. It was only through control and strength that a vampire could survive. The weak were lucky to last a year.

Her undead customers and students would tell her the truth of what had happened to Marisa, and then she could help Leo with those portraits.

But not before sundown tomorrow. She could very easily get the sketches done before dawn and leave them at the bar door, but if he insisted on taking them from her hand he would have to wait. She'd only told him she'd consider meeting earlier to get him off her back.

The hours after Leo left passed quickly, and Abby busied herself cleaning up behind the bar. She might've spent some of that time in her office, taking care of the tedious paperwork that went along with owning a business. But she remained behind the bar, keeping an eye on her customers, wondering if one of them was a murderer. As the hour grew late the human patrons left, one or two at a time. The vampires watched those remaining humans very closely, willing them to leave, waiting for the moment when they could have the bar to themselves. Those few lagging customers began to instinctively realize that they were not wanted. They squirmed. Now and then they glanced with trepidation to the silent and too-still group that remained. Remy's repertoire changed from country tunes to pure jazz, his fingers flying over the keys with inhuman speed. By one-thirty there wasn't a human left in the place.

Margaret locked the main entrance after the last mortal patron departed, and then she turned to blatantly admire the piano player. The sole barmaid in this establishment was a young vamp who listened intently to Abby's lessons. She did her job well, but had an annoyingly obvious crush on Remy, a crush she didn't even attempt to hide. The piano man continued to play, but the tune he switched to after the last of the humans had gone was softer. Gentler. The notes drifted through Abby's blood, and if she was not so angry she'd take great pleasure in the tune.

The vampires who remained looked at Abby expectantly, waiting for her to fetch the blood and warm it properly. This was what they'd been waiting for, after all. A safe feeding. Nourishment. The blood they craved.

Instead of going to the back room for the pigs' blood, she walked around the bar and confronted them all. She lifted a single hand and Remy instantly stopped playing. The sound of the last note hung in the air for a moment, reverberating.

"One of my clientele has been killed," Abby said, her voice even and cold. She looked from one face to the next, searching for a clue. She couldn't see visions from the minds of those like her, only from humans, so the thoughts of her vampire customers were black to her. She searched for signs that one or more of them had recently fed well on human blood, but they all looked hungry. They were all anxious for the pigs' blood, twitching with need, in some cases. If one among them had drained a woman last night that would not be the case. Unless he or she was a very good actor.

It was Charles who looked expectantly from face to face. "We're all here, so you must be talking about a human. What's the big deal? They don't exactly have a long shelf life."

Charles could see snippets of the near future, when he put forth the effort. Usually he misused his gift to choose the mortal women who could give him what he wanted—easy sex and nourishment. He hadn't killed, though, at least not to her knowledge. Charles, with his long, fair hair and pretty face, had been handsome as a human and was even more so as an immortal. The life agreed with him; he embraced it.

And he was annoying her. "Short *shelf life* or not, it is against the rules to kill my customers."

He lifted his hands in easy surrender. "Just saying, boss."

"It couldn't have been one of us," Margaret argued. "I mean, why? We have food aplenty, thanks to you."

Remy nodded his head in agreement. "No one here would dare, Abigail." With his Cajun accent he made the statement sound easy, nonchalant. But there was a fire behind his eyes. Did he believe what he said? His eyes met hers, but she couldn't decipher any alternate meaning there.

But they had a point. It was a relief to be able to believe that whatever had happened to Marisa had not originated here, in her place. As Charles had pointed out, all of her regulars were present tonight, each and every one of them, and they were anxious to be fed.

Remy, Margaret, Charles, Gina, Dalton—a dozen more. So, had a rogue vampire killed Marisa or had a human done the deed?

Humans could be as deadly and merciless as any monster.

She knew *that* all too well.

Chapter 2

After the vampires had been fed they peeled away from the place, one by one, or two by two. Abby cleaned, allowing Margaret to help for a little while before she sent the blonde on her way. When the bar was in good shape, ready for the next day's business, Abby left by the rear door. A very short walk from that back door sat a small, eight-unit apartment building that wasn't much to look at. It was boxy and faded, as plain as any structure could be. She owned it. For now, that sad-looking beige building was home. Upstairs she'd knocked out a couple of walls and had converted the entire second floor into a very nice place. The building might not look like much on the outside, but beyond those walls the rooms were not at all ordinary.

Margaret and Remy each leased an apartment down-stairs, and the other two units were usually rented out to a vamp passing through. A couple of times she'd leased to humans, but they never stayed very long. They didn't know what was wrong with their new home, but their instincts warned them to get out. And they did.

She hadn't taken three steps away from the back door when an unexpected voice startled her.

"I don't suppose you have those sketches yet."

Abby spun around. Leo Stryker stood in shadow, but she should've sensed him there the moment she'd opened the door. The news of Marisa's murder had her rattled. She never got rattled these days. The fact that a human could surprise and even unnerve her was annoying.

"No, I don't." She gathered her composure. "I believe I told you I'd have them for you tomorrow."

The detective stepped out of the shadows. "You did. I just thought I'd take a chance. It never hurts to ask."

"Have you been waiting all this time?" she asked, re-alizing, as she voiced her question that if he'd been here for hours, so close, she would've known it. She would've felt his presence.

Leo shrugged his shoulders. "After I left here I went to the office for a while. I did a bit of research online, read the medical examiner's report for the umpteenth time, and studied crime scene photographs I'll never be able to get out of my head. I was on my way home, passing by the Sundown Bar, and something just… pulled me in."

Marisa's murder was indeed important to Leo, but when he'd turned into Abby's parking lot he had not had murder on his mind. Murder was his business; he'd come here for the purpose of forgetting that nasty business for a while.

They were alone in the dark, without Remy's music, without the rumbling conversation and laughter of a room full of people—and vampires. It was easy to reach into Leo's mind and see what he really wanted, what he always wanted. Her.

"Why me?" she asked.

"Those sketches…"

"You're not here to ask me about the sketches," she interrupted. "You're not here to investigate Marisa's murder at all."

In the darkness she could see Leo much more clearly than he could see her. His eyes were lively. His face was friendly and determined at the same time, if that were possible. Had she unknowingly done something to draw him to her? She could and had mesmerized human males in order to get what she wanted and needed from them, but she had *not* used her influence on this man. If only she could use her sway to make him disappear, to repulse him…and then the truth hit her. She could do just that, could've done it at any time over the past three months, and yet she hadn't. She didn't now.

"I want to know why you won't go out with me," he said. "There's not another man, I know that."

"How could you possibly know there's no other man in my life?"

"You live alone, and there's never any guy hanging possessively around you at the bar. I thought for a while maybe you and Remy had a thing going, but I've seen you two together and you don't act like a couple. You're good friends, I suspect, but there's not a hint of jealousy from either one of you and you rarely touch. Besides," he confessed, smiling gently, "I asked Margaret."

The last thing she needed was a cop taking an interest in her. If he started asking questions, if he got too curious, she'd have to move from this place long before she was prepared to. She liked it here in Budding Corner; she liked her home and her business, and while there was always another home and another bar down the road, she liked this one and wanted it to last. How was she going to get rid of Leo? The truth was disturbing; she didn't want to hurt him. She would *not* hurt him.

But if he learned what she was…

"Lunch," he said. "That's easy enough and really can't be considered romantic."

"No."

"A picnic by the lake," he suggested, undaunted. "More romantic, I suppose, but totally innocent."

Abby took a step toward Leo, drawn by his scent and his throat and his heartbeat and the arousing images in his mind. She was a vampire, but she was also a woman, and occasionally she was beset with a woman's needs and desires. It was a weakness to crave more than blood from a man, and yet she did crave. Humans were food, they were occasionally suitable for entertainment, they were pets, at best. What she was experiencing at this moment went against everything she taught; everything she believed. To become too closely involved with humans meant the very real possibility of exposure. Knowing that didn't make her want Leo any less.

"Innocent?" she said. "I do not think you want innocent from me."

His heart rate increased. She heard and felt it. He blushed, a little, the blood rushing into his face. And lower.

"Tell me what you really want," she whispered as she stopped directly before him. Her hand rose and rested lightly on his chest. Beneath the jacket and shirt and tie she felt his lovely heartbeat. She leaned into him, rested her cheek on his shoulder, moved her lips toward the throb in his throat, testing her own control. "You don't want lunch." A need she had not experienced in a long time sprang to life in an unexpectedly strong way. There was no bar between her and Leo now, no audience of humans and vamps watching. Her own body never throbbed, not in the way it once had, but so close, so very close, she felt a growing and urgent need to take what she should not from this man who was so eager to give it. "You don't want to take me on a picnic. You don't want lunch. This is what you want, isn't it?"

Abby kissed Leo's throat gently. She could almost taste the blood that raced beneath his skin, and she craved it. She had not yearned so desperately for the warmth of human blood on her tongue in a very long time; she took a taste when she could and she enjoyed it, but she did not yearn. And now she was overcome with excitement and craving and desire. She was being swept away; she was losing control. This was like being new and desperately hungry, but she *did* have control and she exercised it now.

Leo wrapped his arms around her and moved her— danced her—into the deeper shadows at the back of the bar. He took her head in his hands and kissed her, and she let him. It had been a long time since Abby had been kissed, and she liked it. She'd missed this sort of touch, the loss of control, the soaring passion. The kiss was more powerful than she remembered any kiss being, more moving and arousing as their lips moved in a magnificent rhythm.

She tasted Leo's tongue as it speared into her mouth. He was so warm he felt hot to her, and she knew that to him she would feel cool. Did he like her cool skin or did it repulse him? Did he think it odd or was he already beyond rational thought? He did not kiss like a man who was repulsed. Whatever restraint he'd been exercising was gone, and the images in his mind came fast and furious. They were chaotic and powerful and primitive, and she knew without question what he wanted.

"You want to be inside me," she said, her lips still touching his.

He didn't respond verbally, but his mouth found her throat and he suckled there as he pushed her skirt high with the intention of removing her panties, only to discover that she wore none. She felt his response and it moved her; his passion, his need rushed through her, as well as through him. They shared a fine, lightning moment of desire and need that wiped away everything else. She lowered the zipper of his trousers and reached inside to touch him, to free him.

Blood flowed to his penis, making it hard and hot, and she wanted it in a way she had not wanted anything for a very long time. She craved the heat and the connection, she wanted the pleasure she'd denied herself for a very long time. She trembled with need.

So did he.

In one smooth motion he lifted her, and she wrapped her legs around him. A muscular man, he did not stumble under her weight or prop her against the wall, but held her steady without any additional support. She liked that he was strong, in body, as well as in heartbeat and desire. He was a fitting partner for a strong woman who had been without male companionship for so many years she could not begin to count them.

Clutching one another, close to coming together and yet enjoying the delicious anticipation of what they knew was to come, they kissed again. Leo's tongue speared into her mouth and Abby rocked her hips, bringing him closer, teasing them both, reveling in the unexpected desire he had brought to life within her.

Leo suffered a troubling thought, an image that flitted through his mind, unwanted but important. She soothed his fears without waiting for him to adjust his stance and fumble in his wallet for the condom he thought he needed.

"I can't have children," she whispered.

That news came as a relief to Leo, as he did not wish to pause what had begun. Unable to wait any longer he pushed inside her, filled her, pumped into her hard and fast. The sensation of being joined was startling and sharp and wondrous and warm, so warm. She had forgotten the intensity of the pleasure of sex; she had forgotten the sheer force of the urges that drew a man and a woman together. She rode him as hard as he pushed into her, hanging on, reveling not only in the physical sensations but in the images in his head. At this moment she was not a teacher, not a leader. She was just a woman taking pleasure from a man. Completion teased her and she slowed, not wanting this moment to be over too soon.

She felt Leo throughout her body, she felt him completely, in an intense rush of pleasure that usually only came to her when she took blood. If she could have both…oh, if she could have both….

With that thought Abby came, the orgasm washing over her with unexpected ferocity. She cried out, she shook, and unable to control herself she lowered her mouth to Leo's throat. A kiss, a lick, and then, as he found his own release, she extended her fangs and bit down.

Blood poured over her tongue, and she tasted not only that warm, nourishing blood, but the power of Leo's pleasure. They were joined entirely, in mind and body, by blood and by lust. He pounded into her and she sucked at his throat, drawing his life into her, tasting all that he was. The world he lived in was filled with colors and beauty and life. She felt that life, she smelled and tasted it.

Leo took a couple of unsteady steps and rested her body and his against the back wall of her bar. He gasped; he panted; he did not release her as she continued to feed. One more sip, one last gulp. And then one more.

Abby felt the weakness that washed over him and she jerked her head away, removing her fangs from his delicious throat. She leaned in for a lick that would cause the wound to heal quickly, but she couldn't allow herself more than that. What had she done? Instead of enjoying a taste she'd latched on and taken nearly twice as much as she should've. If she'd had less control she might've drained him while he was still inside her.

His breath came hard, he shook a little, but he held her. This was what he'd dreamed of, she knew. He'd fantasized about just such an encounter, but she wondered if he'd ever expected they would end up here, like this. She certainly had not. Tempted to distraction by a human. How awkward.

Abby knew what she had to do. For Leo, this encounter could not have happened. She would remember him for a very long time, perhaps forever, but he had to forget it all. It was easy enough. All she had to do was look into Leo's eyes and push at his mind, and he'd forget. The conversation, the kiss, the sex…the fact that she'd drunk from his throat…the fact that he wanted her at all…all gone.

"You're amazing," he said, his voice husky. "I always knew you'd be amazing, I knew it from the first time I saw you. Now that I have you I'm not going to let you go. Take me home with you."

"No."

"Then come back to my place. It's pretty much a shithole, but…"

"I can't."

"I want you again," he said, his voice all but growling.

And she wanted him, much more than she should. She'd tried to turn his mind away from such thoughts, but perhaps that was impossible while they were still joined and shaking. An incredible thought crossed her mind. Could she keep him for a while? Could she make Leo a lover? Feed from him gently, take the pleasure he offered her, be not alone? With a human? Romantic bonds among vampires were not unknown, though they were fairly rare. Sexual partnerships were much more common, but they did not normally last more than a hundred years or so. And here she was actually considering forming such a bond with a mortal man?

What a terrible idea. In a completely illogical way she wanted Leo to forever remember what had happened here tonight, she wanted him to remember *her*, but if he did then he'd show up night after night, and she would not be able to resist him. At this rate she'd end up killing him within a month.

"Put me down," she said.

He did, reluctantly, and when she stood before him she took his face in her hands and looked him in the eye. She stared well past the eyes, into the heart and soul and mind of him. Without words she commanded him to go home, to take a shower and wash the scent of her off of his skin. She ordered him to go to bed and forget what had happened. Reluctantly, more reluctantly than she liked, she commanded him to forget the way he wanted her.

This man was too tempting for her to keep, even for a little while; he was the kind of man who could ruin the orderly life she'd made for herself.

Leo pulled into the driveway of his rented house, foggy-brained and exhausted. He glanced at the clock on the dashboard before turning the key and shutting down the engine. Where the hell had the night gone?

He stumbled a bit on his way to the dark front porch, but quickly regained his footing. Should've left a light on, he supposed. Hell, he was exhausted, and the days to come weren't going to be any better. He was determined to catch the man who'd killed Marisa Blackwell. No one should have to die that way. He was far from perfect, as his ex-wife had been so fond of reminding him, but he did his job well. Maybe he occasionally forgot a birthday or brought the job home with him, but he was who he was, and he couldn't always leave that at the door. Catching bad guys and locking them away was his calling. Once he got his teeth into a case he didn't let go. With that thought he instinctively raised a hand to his throat.

Inside the house he dropped the case file on a table in the hallway and headed for the bathroom, craving a hot shower as if it would wash the stink of the day off of him. He stripped unconsciously, bathed quickly and stepped out to dry himself off. His mind went to Abby Brown, as it too often did, and he realized that there was no reason for him to be so obsessed with her. She'd made it clear she wasn't interested, so he'd move on. The world was filled with women and Abby Brown wasn't any more special than any other. He might as well just give up where she was concerned.

He crawled into bed and closed his eyes, and right before he drifted off his mind took a sharp turn. Abby Brown was special. She was the kind of woman who was worth fighting for. And he was willing to do battle for her.

* * *

Abby hadn't been inside her apartment long when someone knocked gently on the door. Not Remy, she knew from the hesitant knock. Certainly not Leo, who should be sound asleep by now, dreaming of other, more suitable women. She answered the door to find Margaret in the doorway. The pretty girl looked over Abby's shoulder as if she expected to see someone there.

"I'm alone," Abby said.

"Oh. I was sure I smelled a man." She looked at Abby and her eyes went wide. "But that's none of my business. That's not why I'm here."

"Why *are* you here?" Abby stepped back and gestured for Margaret to enter.

"I'm worried about what you asked us about tonight." Margaret wrung her hands. "The poor dead girl who was in the bar last night, Marisa. I hate to think that maybe one of us killed her."

"So do I."

"I mean, she was human, but she was pretty nice most of the time. She left good tips. Most of the young girls don't leave good tips at all."

Abby sighed.

Margaret sat on Abby's long, sunset-colored sofa. The reddish-orange was bright, a flash of color in a world where to watch the sun set was impossible. The young vamp didn't need to rest, not anymore, and yet there were times Margaret seemed to forget that she was no longer human. In time, all that was left of her humanity would fade, and she'd be happier for it. Not yet fifty years old, Margaret was still learning.

"It could've been another human, I suppose, and if a vampire did the deed he could've been, you know, passing through. But I was wondering, if there's a rogue vampire, won't he come to us eventually? Won't he be drawn to us the way Charles and Dalton were?"

"Possibly."

"He could just as easily kill one of us, couldn't he?"

"I suppose he could, but no vamp, no matter how hungry he might be, would feed on another vampire if there was any other choice." Immortality and invulnerability did not go hand in hand.

"But some vamps do…"

"Our blood is cold," Abby said sharply. No vampire should have such fear as this one did. "It would nourish but would not be particularly tasty. Vampires only kill other vampires when there's a feud of some kind, a slight or an insult."

"But vampires do sometimes feed on one another during, you know, sex."

"That's different."

"I know." Again, Margaret fidgeted.

"Don't worry," Abby said. "If a rogue comes to us, he comes. He or she, I should say. However, if the vampire who killed Marisa Blackwell is truly rogue he's already moved on to another town and another victim." The creature who'd sucked Marisa dry wouldn't come to Abby's place hungry for pigs' blood.

"I hope you're right. I wouldn't want anyone to get hurt, especially not Remy."

Abby had to fight to contain her smile. "Remy can take care of himself."

"Yeah, he can." Margaret dipped her head. "Okay, I know I shouldn't say anything, but I admire you. You're my hero, really you are, and to see you take up with a human, it breaks my heart, it truly does."

"That's none of your business," Abby snapped.

"I know that, but I had to warn you. I'm not the only one who sees the way Leo Stryker looks at you. Charles commented on it tonight, right before he left. He said it wasn't fitting for a vampire in your position to be so soft on a human. Using them is one thing, but to truly be friendly just never works. Maybe Charles is jealous, I don't know, but he doesn't like that cop at all. And unless you scrub the smell of him off your skin I'm not going to be the only one to know that you've taken it a step further." She looked up and wrinkled her nose slightly. "He's not like the others, the humans who are so easy to manipulate. We all see it, so surely you do, too. I like it here. I don't want to leave, not yet. If you end up killing a cop we'll all have to disappear in the night, and that will cause a stir. That was the first lesson you taught me. Be invisible, you said."

"I'm not going to kill Stryker."

"How can you be sure?" Margaret fidgeted on the sofa. "The first guy I slept with after I turned, I swear, I couldn't help myself. I sucked the poor fella dry before I knew what I was doing, and it was so damn *good*. I thought I'd do better the second time around, but it didn't work out too well. Not for him, at least. That's one of the reasons I'm determined to confine my romantic relationships to those of my own kind, from here on out."

Meaning Remy, of course.

Abby walked closer to the blonde on the couch. "I am not a fledgling who can't control myself. I have no intention of killing anyone, least of all a cop, nor do I intend to let him, or anyone else, get too close." She leaned down and placed her face uncomfortably close to Margaret's. "And my personal life is none of your concern."

As soon as Abby backed away, Margaret jumped up and headed for the door. "Sorry. I really do have the best of intentions. I think you and I could be friends eventually. We have so much in common, after all."

Abby had friends across the world, but none so young or naive as this one.

When Margaret was gone, Abby stripped of the clothes that still smelled of Leo, only to discover that she herself smelled of him even more strongly. In this one instance, Margaret was right. Leo was different.

Chapter 3

Leo woke with a killer headache. If not for the fact that the murder investigation was so new, he'd call in sick—and he never took a sick day. Lying in bed, barely awake and trying to still the pounding in his head, he wished he could get the image of the dead girl out of his mind. He'd seen the bodies of murder victims before, but they hadn't been anything like this one. Marisa Blackwell had been mutilated, she'd been ripped apart. Swear to God, it looked as though someone had chewed her up and spit her out.

Headache or not, he had people to question today, and he'd be picking up those sketches from Abby Brown. If the sketches were crap he'd bring an ABI sketch artist into her bar and they wouldn't leave until she gave a decent description. Budding Corner didn't have much of a police force; much of a police force wasn't called for, on most occasions, but the Alabama Bureau of Investigation had made their resources available for this case. In a couple of days, ABI investigators would arrive to take over the case, if he didn't solve it before then. As much as he appreciated good help, Leo wanted the murderer in custody before someone arrived to take the case away from him.

In spite of the details of the gruesome case that filled his thoughts, his mind turned to the pleasure of seeing Abby Brown again. Why the hell did he so look forward to spending time with her when she'd made it clear she didn't want to have anything to do with him? A niggling thought teased him. She wasn't worth the trouble. She really wasn't all that good-looking or special or tempting. There were better women out there, women who would give him the time of day. A moment later he rejected those thoughts. The divorce had messed him up more than he'd realized, that was the only explanation. He'd been newly single for two years, transplanted here in this small town for a little more than three months, and instead of getting on with his life he'd gotten fixated on a woman who'd made it clear he was *not* her type.

Why was he so certain she was wrong about that?

Messed up or not, he wasn't waiting until tonight to get those sketches. He knew where Abby lived, after all.

His rented house, the one he kept telling himself was temporary even though he'd made no attempt to find another place, had two small bedrooms and one

ancient bathroom. Still, there were a couple of benefits
to the place. While he remained in the city limits,
barely, the house was remote. He'd never lived in such
a quiet place, and he was discovering that he liked the
silence. On this crisp autumn morning he heard a few
birds, a chirp that might be a chipmunk, and now and
then he heard the wind rushing through the trees that
surrounded the house. Peaceful moments had been few
and far between before his move to Budding Corner.

One other benefit was that the shower had great water
pressure. He stood beneath the spray for a long time,
letting it pound his face and chest as he thought about the
day to come. This morning he had paperwork to take care
of, calls to make to the state forensics lab and to the ABI,
and there were a couple of Marisa's friends he still wanted
to talk to. After that, he was going to drop in on Abby
Brown. He smiled. She wasn't going to like him showing
up unannounced, but that was too bad. He had the high
ground, here. This was a murder investigation, after all.

Logic made Mike and Jason the prime suspects. If
Marisa had been drugged, strangled, beaten, raped or
any combination of those sad possibilities, that's where
he'd concentrate his investigation. But there was something about the way Marisa had been murdered that
screamed of more than the usual sickness. Something
darker. He was going to pursue the two men Marisa and
Alicia had met in Abby Brown's bar, but they weren't
the end of the investigation. They were just a small part
of it. What had made Marisa Blackwell tick? Why had
she spent so many work nights at a—apologies to
Abby—seedy bar? Marisa had a job answering phones

in a small car dealership, so her mornings started early enough. Alicia's hours at a downtown boutique were more flexible, but still, these girls had jobs. If Mike and Jason had been the ones to kill Marisa, why had Alicia gotten off without a scratch? No, there was something else going on.

Leo drove past the Sundown Bar on his way to the station. The neon lights were off; the parking lot was empty. His eyes shot to the building where Abby lived. It wasn't much to look at, but he was in no position to make judgments in that regard.

The police station was located in one of the newer buildings in Budding Corner, but it wasn't much to look at, either. It was as square and boxy as the blustery mayor, and had about as much personality. The people who worked there were nice enough. They were dedicated to their jobs, if not the most brilliant among law enforcement. They were good, down-home folks who were well-intentioned, but not exactly what anyone would call razor sharp.

Maybe that was why Leo hadn't made any but the most casual of friends in the past three months. He didn't fit in here; he wasn't one of them. In fact, he felt most at home in Abby Brown's bar. What did it say about him that he was most comfortable in the company of a woman who was a constant source of rejection?

He dismissed Abby Brown from his mind as best he could, and set about working the case. When it came to his personal life he wasn't particularly sharp himself, but when it came to asking questions and separating the truth from the bullshit, he was a star.

* * *

When the doorbell rang, Abby ignored it. Now and then people got lost, or a man in an unattractive uniform made a delivery to a wrong address. Eventually whoever it was would go away. She was nicely settled on the long reddish-orange couch that dominated the great room where she spent her sleepless days. Since she was alone, and since her skin was so sensitive, she didn't bother with clothes. Why should she? True, her flesh was all but invulnerable, as long as she stayed out of the sun, but with her heightened senses came an increased sensitivity to touch, to the flow of fabrics across her skin. The caress of silk, or of a properly used hand, was heavenly. The rasp of coarse material or an unskilled touch was bothersome.

Her incredible sensitivity also made sex beyond pleasurable. Until last night, she'd denied herself. How would she continue to deny her urges when the memory was so sharp?

This apartment was her haven. When she wasn't in the bar she spent most of her time in this great room. There was also a huge bedroom she rarely used—which at this moment seemed a real pity—and a fabulous kitchen that was a waste of space. There were also two largish guest bedrooms. Not that she had many guests, but she knew vampires all over the world and some of them, a rare few, she called friends. It didn't hurt to be prepared for company, even if she only had a guest every fifty years or so. One never knew when a friend might show up looking for sanctuary.

When she'd remodeled she'd had to keep reselling

in mind, since she couldn't stay in one place for more than fifteen years or so—and that was lucky. More than one bedroom was called for with that in mind, as was the kitchen.

The doorbell rang again. Persistent sucker.

This great room was filled with bookcases heavy with books, a large wide-screen HDTV, and an expensive CD player, along with an impressive collection of CDs, and a sleek, new laptop computer. She didn't sleep and couldn't go outside while the sun shone, and she had to have some way to pass the daylight hours. Too bad she couldn't keep Leo around for entertainment. The idea made her smile. Think of the ways they could pass the day if she had him here.

Her smile faded. If she didn't kill him. It was too late for those thoughts, since just last night she'd nudged him away from her, mentally. He wouldn't find her attractive any longer. He likely wouldn't bother to come into the bar at all, once his investigation was over.

The doorbell rang again, and this time it was followed by a deep voice she recognized. "Come on, Abby. I know you're in there. Time to wake up, sleepyhead. I need those sketches."

In a huff she leaped from the couch, grabbing a silky length of decorative fabric in swirls of red and orange and hot pink. She wrapped the soft fabric around her body and stepped to the door.

"Go away!" she shouted.

There was a short pause before Leo said, "No, I don't think so. I've talked to everyone I can without those sketches. Come on, it's almost three in the afternoon. You can't still be asleep."

She knew what angle the sun would be at, this time of day, this time of year. There was also a large silver maple right outside the door, still fully leafed even though September had arrived weeks earlier. Opening the door would not be painful or dangerous as long as she stayed away from the threshold. With a surge of anger she swung the door in to reveal a tall, too tempting, much-too-curious man.

"What do you want?" she asked, taking care to keep the door more closed than open and to keep herself away from any creeping sunlight.

"Sketches."

"You can collect them tonight," she snapped.

Leo looked her up and down, taking in the length of fabric that covered the parts of her that had to be covered for minimal decency's sake and not much more. The same sorts of mental images she'd caught from him last night reappeared. His mind was not entirely on solving his case. Dammit, he should not be thinking of her this way. She'd done what she could to persuade him to forget his obsession.

"Aren't you going to invite me in?" he asked casually.

"Do you need an invitation?"

"I'm a cop, Abby. Yes, I need an invitation. Please?"

She sighed, stepped back, and allowed the door to swing farther open. "Come in, Detective Stryker."

In his entire life, Leo had never seen anything as tempting as Abby Brown wrapped in a length of thin, colorful fabric. And, quite obviously, nothing else. The fabric clung to her curves, it gaped in interesting places. It barely covered her ass. If he had even a little bit less control he'd be drooling.

Why was a woman like this one alone? Instinctively he glanced toward a door that might—or might not—lead to her bedroom. *Was* she alone? Or did she keep her secrets well?

"How well do you know Remy Zeringue?"

Her eyebrows arched slightly. "Remy? I've known him for years. Why?"

"Marisa's friends say she had it bad for Remy, and a couple of them think they might've been meeting on the sly."

For an instant Abby looked alarmed, and then the telling expression passed. Too late. She was surprised by that tidbit of information.

She recovered quickly. "Remy never mentioned Marisa, though he is a bit of a flirt, I suppose, and I can't say he's never taken a female customer home. You're welcome to ask him about it tonight, of course."

"I stopped by his place downstairs," Leo said. "He didn't answer his door, either." A thought he didn't like occurred to him. What if the piano player was here? What if Remy Zeringue was in the bedroom, the reason Abby didn't have on a stitch of clothing? He'd watched them together and had dismissed the idea that they might be involved, but too many women were suckers for a long-haired, brooding musician with a Cajun accent who called every woman he met *chère* or *darlin'*. "Mind if I look around?"

Abby gave him an unfriendly smile and gestured with her hand. "Be my guest."

She gave him the nickel tour. The apartment, or rather *apartments,* sprawled. The rooms were large and nicely furnished. She liked red and orange, apparently, but there was one nice-size guest room decorated in teal and green and blue, and another was dominated by shades of lavender. In every room the windows were entirely covered with heavy drapes. Not a hint of sunlight broke through. There was enough artificial light to illuminate the rooms well, but it was odd, not to have at least one window opened on such a pretty day.

The master bedroom was huge, dominated by a neatly made king-size bed covered with a silky red bedspread and dotted with orange and hot pink pillows in various sizes. There was no Remy, no sign of a man at all, in sight. The framed oils on the walls were nice, florals featuring poppies and roses, an autumn scene filled with flame-leafed trees. He was staring at that one when he noticed the initial in the bottom right hand corner. *A.* Nothing else, just an ornate, flourishing, *A.* When he glanced around again he noticed that all the paintings were signed the same way. *A.*

"Yours?" he asked, gesturing to the paintings.

"Yes."

"You're good."

"Thanks to years of practice," she responded coolly.

She didn't look old enough to have had years of practice at anything. The information he had on Abby Brown listed her as twenty-eight, but she could easily pass for a college student. Her skin was perfect, if pale, her light green eyes bright, her body fine, petite and still curvy… He shouldn't go there.

"Do you suspect that Remy killed Marisa?" Abby asked softly, and though she tried to hide it, he heard the pain in her voice.

"I don't know," Leo said. "I hope not."

"Why?"

"Because he's your friend and it'll hurt you if he's the one."

She looked to be genuinely surprised by his answer. "You should not care about my feelings. I'm nothing to you, as you are nothing to me."

The words were unusually formal and harsh, but he didn't think it was Abby's intention to be hurtful. She spoke her mind plainly. She was logical and a little confused. He had a sudden and vivid image of Abby laid across her bed, the bright silky fabric around her, beneath her, but not covering her. He could see, so clearly, his body and hers coming together. Hell, he could almost feel her around him, as if the sensation of entering her were a memory, not a fantasy.

"I wish you would not do this to me," she whispered.

"Do what?"

"I'm strong, stronger than you know, but I am not as strong as I should be."

"Who says you have to be strong?"

She didn't answer, but walked to him, dropped the fabric that was all she wore, and without a word began to undress him.

"I'm working," he said halfheartedly. "Nice as this is, I really should…"

"You really should be quiet and help me get these clothes off," she said as she pushed his jacket to the floor. "They are in my way."

Leo wasn't a complete idiot. He did as he was told.

Abby's hands were cool and insistent. Her long, dark hair was loose; it fell across her cheek as she glanced down to unbuckle his belt and unfasten his pants, hiding her expression from him. Was she as anxious as he was? That appeared to be the case. What the hell was happening?

He was a fool to ask questions when everything he'd wanted from Abby Brown was happening right now. Her hands were quick and gentle, her face revealed her hunger for him. Naked and needful, she looked oddly delicate, and he wanted nothing but to give her everything she wanted of him, and more. She wasn't shy; her hands were everywhere. She even licked her lips as she peeled away his clothes.

He was so caught up in the moment he almost forgot about the condom in his wallet. With a jerk of his hand he reached for his pants, but Abby's surprisingly strong fingers on his wrist stopped him from moving too far. And then she pulled him onto the bed, where they both bounced gently and his body pressed to hers.

"You don't need it," she whispered. "I cannot have children and we are both healthy."

"How do you know I'm healthy?"

She arched beneath him, wrapped her legs around his hips, brought them closer together. "I know," she said softly, "because I have powers beyond those of normal human beings. I can see into your body and your soul, I can see who you are and right now what you want and what I want is the same."

"Kinky," he said. "I like it." And she moved against him and wiped out every thought.

Her skin was cool and smooth and perfect. She smelled like cinnamon and sex and vanilla. Cookies. She smelled like cookies. He kissed her shoulder, wondering if she would taste as sweet as she smelled. His lips lingered on her perfect flesh. No, she didn't taste like cookies; she tasted like woman.

He was so close to being inside her it was driving him crazy, but he waited. For months he'd dreamed of this moment, and now that he had Abby wrapped around him he wasn't going to rush; he wasn't going to waste this opportunity. He smoothed her hair away from her face and kissed her throat. She gasped, moaned in pleasure. She responded intensely to his touch, and he liked it. He wanted to make her his in every way. His hands skimmed over her body, stopping here and there to explore and arouse.

Abby moved like a snake, undulating against him, rubbing her body against his, bringing them closer to the end. He'd pursued her for months and she'd denied him, but now that they were here it seemed she had less patience than he did. She caught her breath in a sigh of intense pleasure and wanting. She threw her head back and arched her spine. Maybe he was willing to be patient and take his time, but she obviously was not.

He pushed inside her, filled her, eased the ache that had been driving him crazy since she'd opened the door and presented herself to him barely covered by that length of brightly colored fabric. He'd thought of having her in just this position a thousand times, but even his imagination hadn't been as remarkable as the real thing. There were times when he'd thought he'd never get what he wanted from her, never be so close. Now here they were, like a dream come true.

She was oddly cool, inside and out. Her skin, her lips, the inner muscles that quivered against him, all were without the expected heat, as if she were made of gentle frost over silk. No sensation could compare to the delicious combining of his heat and her chill. He was lost in her and there was nothing but the two of them and the pleasure their bodies reached for. She kissed his chest…what the hell, was she biting?…no, no, it was just a kiss. A fervent kiss. As she kissed him her body grew warmer; the chill of her skin subsided, her hips moved faster, more insistently. She stole every thought from his head, until there was nothing but her body and his and the need that drove them.

She came hard, with her lips still latched to his chest, her legs tight around him, their bodies joined…and while she quivered he gave over, too.

They lay spent on her bed, silent but for the sound of his breath. The woman beneath him seemed to make no sound at all, no raspy breathing, no pounding heart. If he didn't know better he'd think she was entirely unaffected.

Nothing had ever drained him so. Abby kissed his chest, she licked him there. Her head was tilted so he could not see her expression, and he wanted very much to see her face.

"I should like to keep you," she whispered.

He bent his head and kissed her shoulder. "I would very much like to be kept."

"Would you, truly?"

"Yes."

She rolled him onto his back with surprising quickness and ease. "I have not shared myself with anyone for such a long time," she whispered. "I crave the sharing as much as the sex, as much as the blood."

Leo's body tensed. "The *blood?*"

She was above him, now, as he had once been above her. Her eyes bore into his and he felt an invasion, as if her gaze was a physical thing that pierced his eyes and traveled into his brain. "You cannot move."

Leo attempted to gently push Abby away and roll from the bed, but she was right. He couldn't move. His limbs were frozen. Had she drugged him? And if so, how? He hadn't drunk or eaten anything since entering her apartment.

But there had been the sting when he'd thought she was biting him. Did she have a needle in this bed? Had she drugged him with a muscle relaxant? Hell, he had the worst taste in women!

"I won't hurt you," she said, and as she spoke she smoothed back a strand of hair at his temple. "When this day is over I will make you forget, but for now…I swear, there is something about you that makes me feel lonelier than I ever have before, something that compels me to cling to you, to tell you the truth of who I am."

"Who are you?" he asked, still confused but no longer afraid. Her words and her voice—and more important her eyes—spoke of loneliness and fear and a need for something he himself craved. Someone to cling to. Though the situation was confusing and should be frightening, he could not be afraid of her. Besides, if she'd meant to hurt him she could've done so by now.

Abby shook back her long, thick hair, and then she looked him in the eye. Softer this time, without demand, without that feeling of invasion. "I was born Abigail Smythe in 1543. My memories of that time are not clear, but I know I was a farmer's daughter on a spot of land in the north of England, who grew to have a passably pretty face and a pleasing manner, both gifts from my mother. My life was simple. I suppose it was happy enough, though to be honest it's hard to remember, after such a long time. It's as though that girl was someone else, someone distant, and yet I realize that foolish, weak girl was me.

"When I was fifteen my father arranged my marriage to an older man who was important in the community. I thought he was quite something, but of course now I know he was nothing more than what today would be called a big fish in a small pond. Mr. Bailey, though nearly as old as my father, was a good and attentive husband until it became clear to him that I was not going to give him the sons he desired. Two of our children were stillborn, both girls, and when I was nineteen I gave him a strong, beautiful daughter. The delivery was difficult and I almost died. After Merry was born I did not conceive again."

Leo knew when people were lying to him; it was part of his job, hell, it was a part of who he was. Everyone had a tell or two, when they were spinning a lie, and he could spot them from a mile away. From all he could see, Abby was not lying. Impossible or not, she believed what she was telling him. Still… "This is not…"

"Possible? I assure you, it is. Listen to me, if you please." She turned her head to gaze toward the heavily curtained window. "The final years of my human life are more clear in my memory than those that preceded them. I was as happy as could be expected, considering that my husband despised me and would on occasion beat me when he found himself longing for the son I could not give him. I had my daughter, a lovely, sweet girl, and I never had to worry about food or shelter. All in all, my life was fine."

Leo felt a surge of anger. Her story was fantastic, it was unbelievable, but there had to be some truth to it, somewhere. "He beat you?"

Abby ignored his question. "When I was twenty-three years old, a young mother and a reluctant wife, a scourge came to our village. People died horrible deaths in the night, and their dry, bloodless bodies were left in the streets for all to see when the sun rose. There was panic, as you can imagine. Town meetings were held frequently. Mr. Bailey was always present at those meetings, of course, as he was a leader in the community. We were told to be vigilant, to be suspicious of everyone, even those villagers we thought we knew. We were warned to be especially cautious at night, as that was when the killings occurred, and not to allow anyone into our homes."

He saw the pain in her eyes; he felt it as if it were his own, as if they remained connected in a way that went well beyond sex.

"But how can you say no to a traveling priest who

arrives at the door, hungry and looking for shelter from the rain, just past dark? How can you turn away a human being in need?" She looked him in the eye. "I did not turn him away. I invited him in, even though my husband was not at home. In a matter of moments the priest who was not a priest at all rendered me immobile, as I have done to you, and I watched as he broke my daughter's neck and drank every drop of her blood. When that was done he turned to me. I begged him to kill me. I did not want to live without my child. Merry was all I had in my life that was good, and I could not continue on without her."

Her voice dropped. "The creature did kill me, but he didn't allow me to remain dead. He brought me back as a vampire, like him. I think if I had not asked him to kill me he would've left me alone, he would've allowed me to remain dead."

Perhaps realizing, or at least suspecting, that he did not believe her, Abby smiled. Two fangs appeared, sharp canines elongating and growing more pointed before his eyes, transforming what should've been a pretty smile on a beautiful face into a demonstration of terror.

And he believed. How could he not? The truth was right before his eyes. "Are you going to kill me?"

"No." The fangs retracted as quickly as they had grown.

What she'd told him was impossible, incredible, but he had no choice but to believe. Beyond the truth he knew, another world existed. A dark, hidden, terrifying world where creatures he'd thought to be mythical existed. Considering some of the nasty murders he'd seen during his career, he couldn't be shocked. He was surprised, however, that Abby was a part of it. She wasn't evil. No matter what she said, he saw who she really was and there was nothing to fear. "What happened next? How did you survive?"

Abby cocked her head and looked at him as if she were confused by his question. Maybe she was just taken aback that he wasn't begging for mercy or shrinking away in horror. "I was crouched in the corner, holding the body of my child, when Mr. Bailey came home. He didn't realize what had happened, of course. When he saw us there he thought I'd somehow killed Merry. As if I would've ever…" She shook her head quickly. "Mr. Bailey rushed toward me. He raised his hand to strike me as he had a thousand times. But this time, I fought back. I pushed against him as hard as I could and he flew across the room. I followed him, angry and grieving and hungry in a way I did not understand. My husband screamed when he saw my face and realized what I had become. He pleaded for mercy when I threw him to the floor with a newly discovered strength. While he cried I pounced upon him and I went for his throat. I drank every drop of Mr. Bailey's sour, old blood, and I liked it." She looked him in the eye. "I am a monster, Leo."

He could not argue with that statement, not if what she told him was true. "Did you kill Marisa Blackwell?"

She shook her head. "No. I haven't killed anyone in a very long time. I can survive quite well on pigs' blood, and by occasionally feeding on humans and then making them forget, as I made you forget last night."

"Last night I…" He got no further before the memory came rushing back, perhaps because she allowed it to return to him. A really great kiss, a quick coupling in the shadows…and more, apparently.

"Other vampires, younger ones, don't always have such restraint. They either kill randomly or subsist on animal blood until they learn to control their strength and their needs. I serve pigs' blood in my bar after hours. I teach those who wish to learn how to survive without giving in to their monstrous urges." Her green eyes went paler than usual, losing almost all their color, for a moment. "It's not as if we can allow people to disappear night after night, it's not as if we can feast on the humans around us and continue to thrive. We do not die easily, but we can die. We can be hurt. It is not in our best interest to make our existence known, and that means keeping the body count down no matter how thirsty we might be. In the name of survival we learn to deny ourselves what we most want, as I have denied myself you, until now."

Four hundred years was such a long time. How many people had Abby killed, before she'd learned the control she spoke of? Was she truly a monster behind the face that had enchanted him? Would a monster "most want" a bond with a human, a connection she confessed she had denied?

"What happened to you, after you changed?" he asked.

Abby dipped her head almost demurely, though he knew she was anything but demure. Long, thick, soft hair hid a portion of her face from him. "My little village was entirely wiped out," she whispered. "There was no one left to tell the tale of what had really happened, so the travelers who found the remains of the carnage blamed the deaths on a terrible disease and burned everything. The vampire who did all the killing survived, of course, as did I and a couple of other fledglings. The others he turned did not last out the year. They weren't strong enough."

"What happened to the creature that killed your daughter and all the others?"

Her eyes narrowed, and he saw in them a hatred that would bring most men to their knees. "I learned a few years later that he called himself Callosus. He was ancient then, a power among powers. He survives still, I know it. I swear, some days I'm sure I can feel him close by, other days…nothing. One day I will find him, and when I do I'll take his head, even if it means losing my own in the process."

He should not believe a word of Abby's fantastic tale, but he did. In the face above him he saw the woman and the monster, the tragedy and the slaughter and the heartache. He saw her heart and the gruesome fiend she was…had been…could be.

He should be terrified, but he wasn't. It occurred to him with more than a touch of humor that Abby Brown, no matter what she'd done, couldn't be much more of a bloodsucker than his ex-wife….

"Why are you telling me this?"

"Because I like you," she said, "even though I should not. You make me feel lonely, when for the past two hundred years I have been more than happy enough to remain alone, to rely on no one but myself, to be solitary in all ways. It's too dangerous to get close to anyone or anything. Every few years I change my last name, though I keep the name Abby or Abigail. That's not much, but it's all I have left of who I once was and I am loathe to let it go entirely. I have been content. I have not killed—I've tried to live my life simply, with no complications, and now…and now here you are, a complication of the worst sort."

Beyond the sad and horrifying story, behind the fangs and the assertion that she was a monster, Leo saw something more. He saw the woman he'd been drawn to from the beginning. She was real. Not exactly as he had believed her to be, not as simple or ordinary, but still, she was real and she was here and there was a reason for this confession.

"You're telling me all this because you want my body," he said wryly.

"In more ways than one," she responded. "The sex is fabulous. I'd forgotten how powerful a man and woman coming together in the name of pleasure could be. And I swear, I want to suck on every vein in your body."

He could not stop the mental image that formed in his mind. "Every one? Have at it."

"Don't be flip," Abby said, slightly angry, still more sad. "It simply can't be. For a few nights, maybe even a few years, perhaps we could make it work. But I would always have to hide the truth from you, feed on you and hope I don't feed too much, take away the memories you cannot keep…"

"I don't want you to take away my memories."

"I know." She caressed his face. She looked into his eyes in that way she had, and suddenly he could move again. He had control of his body once more. Any sane man would leap from the bed and run like hell, but instead Leo took Abby into his arms. He should not believe what she'd told him, but he did. He should be afraid, but he was not. If she'd wanted anything from him that he wasn't willing to give she could've taken it last night, or when he'd shown up at her door. She could've taken him up on any one of his invitations during the past three months and while they were alone she could've done whatever she'd pleased with him.

For now, at least, she didn't want anything other than what he most craved.

Her skin had grown cool again and he tasted it with relish. Not as she had tasted him, to the bone, but still, he feasted.

Chapter 4

Remy met Abby at the door to the Sundown Bar at opening time. He wouldn't start playing for an hour or two, but like her, he was tired of hiding in his apartment. He stood behind her and took a long breath. "Abigail, darlin'," he said, his Cajun accent heavy, even after all his time away from the city where he'd been born—both in body and as a vampire, "you smell like police."

She sighed, unlocked the door and stepped inside. "I showered." Twice.

"He's not just on you, he's in you. He's in your very cells and he's in your veins. Are you sure this is a good idea?"

First Margaret and now Remy! "It's my life to do

with as I please." She glared at him. "It's not like you can criticize. You take up with humans all the time."

"Not policemen." He shrugged his broad shoulders. "Well, policewomen would be more my type, if I were so foolish."

She spun on him. "Marisa Blackwell? For goodness sake, Remy, she was little more than a child!"

His expression was suddenly solemn. "She was no child, I assure you. And since you are so obviously wondering, I didn't kill her."

"You screwed her and fed on her. How am I to know you didn't get carried away and take it all?" Goodness knows she'd been tempted enough to take every drop of Leo's blood.

"I did not," he said softly. "Believe me or don't."

The door swung open and the first of their human customers arrived. There was nothing more to be said, not until much later. "Swear to me," she whispered.

Remy's expression didn't change. "Believe me or don't. I do not beg or swear."

Leo was strangely tired, but he didn't let up as the afternoon turned into night. None of the usual suspects made any sense at all in Marisa Blackwell's case. She hadn't been robbed. She didn't have anything other than the most casual ex-boyfriend. She wasn't into drugs. Her frequent evenings at the Sundown Bar were her only evidence of a wild side, that and her affair with Remy.

She'd told several of her friends about him, though her family had never heard the name. In their eyes she was a sweet, untouched, virginal angel. He didn't bother to disabuse them of that notion, and wouldn't unless it became necessary for the case.

Remy or the elusive Mike and Jason? Someone he had missed entirely? A sociopath passing through town? This case wasn't nearly neat enough to suit him.

In many ways, the piano player was the only suspect that made any sense to Leo. Still, he had no proof and he didn't want Remy to be the one. He wasn't sure why and it didn't matter what he wanted. Between Remy Zeringue or a serial killer—or killers, if that was Jason and Mike's game—with no motive other than "she was there," he'd take Remy any day.

At least tonight he'd get to see Abby when he went by her place to collect the sketches. He'd meant to do that this afternoon, but had never made it over that way. He must be coming down with something. Instead of going to Abby's place and insisting on collecting those sketches she'd promised him, he'd…well, he wasn't sure how he'd gotten so sidetracked, but hours after he'd left the station he'd woken from a long, mind-numbing nap in his car, parked behind the Dollar General Store on the main drag.

He couldn't afford to get sick now, and he had to look beyond Remy. Until he tracked down the men who'd been with Marisa and her friend Monday night, he couldn't settle on anyone as the sole suspect. Some sort of proof would be nice, and at the moment he had none.

He was suddenly assaulted by a craving for cookies.

Abby furiously wiped down the bar, ignoring the stares from humans and vamps alike. She was moving a touch faster than was normal for any human; she knew that and still she couldn't make herself slow down. Let them stare; she didn't care. Her mind was spinning and her body was tense, tight, on fire. It was probably no coincidence that Remy was playing a haunting version of "Crazy" at the moment.

Remy—and others—had often encouraged her to take up with a human or humans in a sexual way. Many vampires kept ignorant mortals as sexual partners, treating them as if they were pets. Abby had dismissed the notion, claiming it was a weakness to need anything from a human beyond blood. She needed no one, least of all something—someone—as fragile as a man.

Her craving for Leo should be satisfied by now. She'd sampled his body and his blood all afternoon; she'd enjoyed pleasure and warm sustenance and even laughter. The bed she never slept in had become a haven for one fine afternoon. And then she'd wiped Leo's mind of their interlude and sent him away.

Abby was now acutely sensitive to Leo, thanks to the blood she'd taken in. When he pulled into the parking lot, she felt his closeness. She knew, before he opened the door to the bar, that he was confused by the missing time and weakened by the loss of blood. And all she wanted was to hold him, take him into her body again, and taste his blood. Just a drop. That would be enough, for now.

Maybe.

Leo smiled wanly as he walked toward her. Every vamp in the place, every one, watched Leo with too interested eyes. Were they made curious by his reaction to her, or by her reaction to him?

"Do you have those sketches?"

"Yes." She reached under the bar and pulled out two pencil drawings of the men she remembered seeing with Marisa and Alicia. Not that they would do him any good. The more she picked from Leo's brain concerning the murder, the more certain she was a vamp had done the deed.

"Thanks." He took a stool, ran fingers through his hair, and reached for the sketches she offered. "Wow, these are great. I didn't know you were such an artist."

Abby's heart broke a little. Just hours ago he'd admired her paintings. After sex, explanations he'd miraculously accepted, and sex once more, he'd asked about the artwork in her bedroom. She'd told him when and where she'd painted them, and what her life had been like at the time. As she'd shared that part of her past, she'd realized that in her most productive years, artistically speaking, she'd been alone. Entirely, completely alone, existing cautiously from one meal to the next, filling the long hours with paint and canvases and strangers who would never remember that they'd met her.

Naturally, Leo remembered nothing of the conversation, which was the reason she'd felt so free with him. If she were so foolish as to have sex with him again, she'd have to tell him once more that she could not have children so he did not need the blasted condom in his wallet. For him, sex with her would always be the first time. There could never be anything resembling a meaningful relationship between them—as if that was possible for any vampire.

"I'm not really an artist," she said. "I dabble. You look beat. How about a nice, tall glass of…"

He stopped her with a raised hand. "On duty."

"Orange juice," she finished with a smile.

He grinned. "Probably not a bad idea. I feel like I'm coming down with something." He studied the drawings. "I fully intended to drop by your place this afternoon and see if these were ready, but I didn't make it." He frowned; wrinkles in his forehead creased. She wanted to soothe him, to explain that he wasn't losing his mind. If she got too close she'd have him back in her bed, and this time she might not let him go.

"I have the oddest craving for cookies," he said. "I don't usually have much of a sweet tooth, but man, I'd kill for a sugar cookie right now."

In the old days she might've chained Leo to her bed and taken what she wanted until she tired of him, and then she'd make him forget everything and release him after he was so dazed and damaged that he no longer appealed to her. These days people did not go missing without causing a stir, especially not a cop. More's the pity. He was so incredibly special and different. She had never known another man like him.

Abby steeled her spine. She was beginning to sound like a human, weak and sentimental, instead of approaching Leo as if she were the monster and he the victim. Did monsters love? Not that she had seen. There was loyalty, in some cases. There was occasionally companionship or friendship or an alliance formed for the sole purpose of self-preservation. But that was not real love. It was part of the price she paid for immortality, for strength, for gifts that no human could ever understand.

Sadly, she realized that she couldn't stay here much longer. Looking at Leo she knew that too well. He would always be a temptation, and she could not afford to be tempted. As soon as Marisa's murder was solved, she'd make arrangements to move on. If she disappeared now, without cause and a modicum of preparation, he would surely consider her a suspect. It wouldn't do for him to chase after her.

"I need to talk to your piano player," Leo said. "Did you know Remy was seeing Marisa Blackwell?"

"No, I didn't. Are you sure?" He'd told her the news this afternoon, but of course he didn't remember.

Remy wasn't above taking a woman home, sleeping with her, and taking what he needed, but like Abby he was old and powerful and had control of his needs. He would never kill to take the blood he required; it was simply unnecessary. He said he hadn't killed Marisa, and she took him at his word. If vampires had souls— and Abby was conflicted about that question—then Remy's was one of the good ones. As long as he had his music and a string of women for sexual entertainment and blood, he was content. He had no reason to kill.

Unless something had broken and he'd lost control. A day ago she would have thought that impossible. Now she had to wonder.

"He doesn't take many breaks," she said. "Can it wait?"

"I suppose." Leo sipped at his juice. She wished she had some decent food to offer him, something to help build back the strength she'd sapped this afternoon, maybe one of the cookies he craved, but all she had was a jar of pickled eggs. Even if she didn't gag at the thought of real food, pickled eggs wouldn't appeal to her at all. There were peanuts, and she casually placed a bowl near Leo. She didn't want him to think she was mothering him, but the man needed some protein. He almost immediately homed in on the nuts, munching, watching the crowd, keeping an eye on Remy—and on her. It was unnerving.

Once again Remy started playing "Crazy."

When Abby couldn't take it any longer she put Margaret in charge and headed down a narrow hall to her office. The room was no better than a glorified closet, and she didn't spend any more time here than she had to, but at the moment it was a place to hide. Vampires shouldn't hide from anyone, least of all an easily influenced human male whose only appeal to her was in his penis and his blood. He was ordinary. He was replaceable. Everyone was replaceable!

But like it or not there was more. She would never forget the way he'd looked at her as she'd spilled her guts about her past, her making, who she was. He'd forgotten, but she had not. Even though she had used her power to immobilize him, even though she had revealed herself as a monster, he'd felt sympathy for her. Not pity; she hated pity. But he had been moved. He'd cared.

And she was an idiot for allowing that to matter.

She felt him coming down the hall, but she didn't hide or run, as she could've. Instead she sat on the edge of her desk and waited. When Leo appeared in her doorway, she attempted a smile.

"What's wrong?" he asked.

"Nothing."

He didn't believe her, that was obvious, but didn't press the issue. "So, when are you going out with me? You can't keep saying no."

"I can," she said gently.

"You don't know me well enough, is that it? Okay, here I am in a nutshell. Thirty-one years old, former homicide detective, current catch-all detective in a podunk town where *usually* nothing much happens. Divorced, no children, no family living close by so I'll never subject you to Sunday dinner with a brother or a cousin or my mother. They're all many, many hours away from here, which is best for all concerned."

"Leo, I…"

"I believe in Jack Daniel's, college football, and I suppose I must believe in love at first sight because I have not been able to get you out of my mind since the first time I walked into this bar."

She did not have a heartbeat to race, but she felt as if her stomach clenched, as if her insides turned to cold stone. "Maybe that's just lust at first sight."

"Maybe," he conceded. "At this rate I'll never find out."

Abby took a deep breath, not because she needed to breathe, but because the action itself was calming. Yes, she had to leave Budding Corner as soon as possible. If necessary she'd find Marisa's killer herself, turn him over or dust him, depending upon his species, and then she'd be able to get out of town and away from this tempting man.

"Would you kiss me?" she asked.

The request took Leo by surprise, she could tell by the expression on his face. "Here and now?"

"Here and now." Perhaps she could not have everything, but that didn't mean she could take nothing at all.

Leo walked into the room with a steady, strong stride. All she could take was a kiss, but she wanted to leave him something to remember. If she took any more blood she might kill him; and she couldn't have sex with him without being driven to take a taste. But a kiss…a kiss wouldn't hurt anyone, and when she disappeared he would have that kiss as a pleasant memory.

And so would she.

It was a test of her strength, to kiss him and take nothing more, but she was strong. She was powerful. She could do it.

Abby sat on the edge of her desk; Leo placed his hands on either side of her and leaned in. As far as he knew this was their first kiss, but he didn't hesitate. His mouth took hers, and she reveled in his warmth and his taste. More than that, she got lost in the emotion of the kiss, the power of connection, even of love, of not being alone in this small world where time flew past and had no end.

Leo's arms gradually and gently worked around her and she stood, pressing her body to his. His hands were in her hair, his heat enveloped her. She did not want the kiss to end, but nothing lasted forever. Nothing.

His hands settled on her hips, slipped around to her backside and pulled her close so she could feel his response. Perhaps instinctively he knew this wasn't a first kiss, maybe he knew her body and his were meant for one another.

Finally, he ended the kiss with a sigh. "You have to go out with me now."

"Maybe tomorrow."

He jerked away from her. "Really? You're not yanking my chain?"

She had such a hard time keeping up with all the new slang and phrases, it changed so fast, but this one she knew. "I am not yanking your chain."

"Lunch?"

"Dinner. I can let Remy and Margaret run the bar for a couple of hours."

"Hot damn." In spite of his exhaustion, he gave her a true smile.

"I have to go back to work."

"Me, too. When can I talk to your piano man?"

She'd been so caught up in the kiss, she hadn't realized that the piano was silent. "Sounds like he's on a break right now."

"Good. Let's get this over with." Leo allowed her to lead the way down the hallway. Everyone, human and vampire, was watching as they walked into the bar from the back room. Remy was nowhere to be seen. Neither was Margaret. One of the regulars, a human who was in the bar at least four nights a week, had taken over behind the bar and was doing an acceptable job, but Abby was furious.

"Where did Remy and Margaret go?" she asked hotly.

"They left a few minutes ago."

"Together?" Leo asked.

"No." An older man who sat in the corner, as usual, responded. "Remy skedaddled, and Margaret took off after him. You know how that girl loves her some Remy."

"I gotta go." Leo leaned down and gave Abby a

warm peck on the cheek. "I'll see you tomorrow night." And then he was gone.

After the door closed behind Leo the bar seemed horribly empty and silent. No music, no laughter from bubbly Margaret. Everyone stared at Abby, and she couldn't blame them. The vampires were surprised that she'd taken up with a human, and the humans had never seen her with a man before.

Abby relieved the customer who'd taken over the bar; she polished a glass that did not need polishing. Where would she go next? Up north, she supposed. Perhaps for a while she'd stay in a place even more isolated than this one. No more caves, no more farms, but there were many places in this big country that were basically off the map. There was also Europe, but it wasn't quite time to head back in that direction.

Though she craved time by herself, time to plan for what might come next, she didn't stay alone for long.

Charles hadn't been in Budding Corner more than a month. He'd gravitated here looking for a peaceful way of life, hoping to learn the control required for a long existence. It wasn't love of a weaker species that made him cautious. Like her, he wanted to exist as peacefully—and invisibly—as possible. He was a pretty boy, with blond hair almost as long as Remy's and amber eyes that had once been dark brown. He had a dry sense of humor but didn't say much. Everyone liked him well enough.

Most vampires had some sort of power that was revealed to them as they came to terms with their new bodies and minds, and Charles was no exception. He saw snippets of the near future, but had not as yet learned to control his power. He was young, still, not much more than seventy years old. Visions came and went, most of them of no concern to an immortal who had no love for the humans. The women he dallied with meant no more to him than the carton a human's milk might come in. He kept them alive, he drank from them carefully without ever revealing who and what he was, but to him they were containers. They were necessary.

"Got yourself a human, I see," Charles said.

"That's none of your business," Abby snapped.

"They are handy," he said, not taking the broad hint. "I remember sex from before the change, and it was pale in comparison to a vampire's experiences. There's nothing at all wrong with having sex with a human, but I suspect you're looking for more from our local detective." He shook his head.

"What do you want?"

Charles shrugged his shoulders, obviously unconcerned. "I just had a vision and it concerns your new friend. I thought you might want to know, but if you don't…"

"Tell me!"

Charles shook his long, pale hair and gave her a tight smile. "All right. The next time you see your cop boyfriend, he'll be dead."

Chapter 5

Leo parked his car in front of his crappy rented house at the edge of town, turned the key to shut off the engine and stepped out, a too thin manila folder clutched in one hand. The night was dark, tree limbs overhung the dirt drive, and his place was so isolated there wasn't another house in sight. He'd thought Budding Corner would be temporary, but since Abby had kissed him… maybe it wasn't temporary after all. He couldn't very well bring her here. She deserved better.

He'd hoped to catch Remy in the parking lot or in his apartment, but had had no luck. For now he'd take another look at the case file, hoping to see something new before the ABI came in and took over. Come hell or high water, he would talk to Remy Zeringue tomorrow.

She was sitting on the front porch steps. He didn't see her right away, since the front porch light was burned out.

"Abby?" How had she gotten here so fast? Why did she look so worried? She stood slowly, and he was shaken by the certainty that something was wrong. She looked different. Something was off. "What are you doing here?"

"I missed you," she said, whispering. Didn't exactly sound like her voice, but then he was tired, and it was late, and nothing was as it should be.

"How did you get here so fast?"

She walked toward him. The usual white blouse and long skirt were damn near painted on her, showing him every curve, every tempting swell. "Shortcut. I ran."

Dressed like that? "But…"

"Don't ask so many questions." She smiled, and he relaxed. "You know what I want."

He knew what *he* wanted, but Abby had never shown much interest in him, until tonight when she'd asked for a kiss and accepted his invitation for a date. When she relented she really relented. Nice.

She walked into his arms, and he quit asking so many questions. Abby was here. He'd be a fool to question that.

She was cool. She squirmed against him as if she could not get close enough. He loved the feel of her, but something was wrong; she didn't smell right. Abby always smelled good, sweet and clean and tasty. At the moment there was something sour about the way she smelled, something wrong. He was about to release her when she lifted her head and kissed his throat. She licked the side of his neck, and he went very still, enjoying the sensation. Maybe the sour smell was coming from the woods; that couldn't possibly be Abby. She took the folder from his hand and dropped it to the ground. He didn't care. Pages fluttered. A gentle wind caught Abby's sketches and took them away.

And then she bit him. He felt her teeth sinking into his skin, the sharp bite of invasion. Too late, he heeded the warning, he heeded the smell. He tried to fight her off, to push her away, to get her the hell away from his throat, but even though she was tiny compared to him, she was stronger than he was, much stronger, with arms and jaws like steel. She held him in place with incredibly, impossibly strong arms while she sucked on his throat. She gurgled; she slurped his blood, and Leo felt the life draining from him. His knees went out, but Abby held him up. His eyes rolled back in his head, and his entire body shuddered. She slammed him to the ground, her face buried in his throat as she sucked the life from his body. He smelled his own blood, as well as the stench that came from her skin. In the midst of the violence a fleeting but coherent thought crossed his mind. Was this the way Marisa Blackwell had died? Had Abby, the woman he had fantasized about and dreamed about and kissed, torn Marisa's throat apart and sucked out her blood? Impossible…and yet here he was.

Dark hair covered his face, blocking out the night's gentle light. Right before everything went black that hair turned to blond.

A trill of laughter that was not Abby's filled the night.

* * *

Abby ran, following Leo's trail, drawing on the connection she had formed with him when she'd drunk his blood. With a vampire's grace and unnatural speed she all but flew, a blur in the quiet neighborhoods, and then beyond, where the homes were far apart and the trees grew thick. Dogs barked. The cool night air washed over her, and she listened, trying to find Leo's heartbeat among all the rest.

There it was. Too slow, too unsteady. A thump. Seconds later another thump. And then…nothing.

She did not stop but continued on. All was quiet. Too quiet. If she'd been able to shed tears, tears would've come. Amazingly, she found she was capable of experiencing deep sorrow, still, after all this time. It hurt. Leo Stryker was a good man and she should've been able to save him.

If she hurried, perhaps she still could.

She ran into the side yard of a small clapboard house, his house, her eyes on the two forms in the dark driveway. Leo lay on the ground, motionless. Dead, as Charles had said he would be. Margaret stood over him, licking her lips, laughing.

"Why?" Abby screamed as she rammed into Margaret and spun the vampire who was warm with Leo's blood back against his car. The metal of the driver's door crunched and crinkled beneath Margaret's weight and Abby's force.

The young vampire laughed. "You're asking me why? Hypocrite. You didn't leave me much. He was barely an appetizer."

"I could've loved him." The words Abby spoke surprised her with their power and their truth.

"He was going to tie Remy to Marisa's death," Margaret argued. "I couldn't allow that."

"Remy can take care of himself!" Abby glanced down at Leo's body, so cold and still and pale. It was wrong; he should be alive and laughing and flirting. He should be on the trail of a killer who'd broken the rules of his world, rules he had sworn to keep. She didn't want to believe it was possible but she had to ask, "Did Remy kill Marisa?"

"Yes," Margaret said. "And no." The young vampire shimmered, and instead of Margaret pinned to Leo's car it was Remy.

Or at least, the form appeared to be Remy until it spoke.

"He was sleeping with her," Remy's body with Margaret's voice said. "Night after night after night. I don't mind that, really, because I knew he was feeding from her. Pigs' blood will do in a pinch, but it doesn't compare to human blood fresh from the donor. But he started to like the twit too much, and I couldn't have that. We're going to be together, Remy and I, as soon as he comes to his senses."

Abby slammed Margaret against the car once more. The figure shimmered, and once again she appeared in her true form. A beautiful monster. "You finally found your gift, I see."

"I did. And isn't it a doozy?" Margaret smiled. "This is really going to come in handy." The vamp's gaze remained steady. She was not afraid—and that was a mistake. "You don't teach the fledglings that to take all the blood from a human is so exhilarating," she said.

"I've tried to adapt, as you have, but I always remembered what it was like in those wonderful, free, early days. When I took the last of Marisa's blood, I was washed in a flood of power. I felt her life inside me, I knew everything, I felt her love for Remy and her confusion that he had killed her, because of course she saw what I wanted her to see, just as your Leo saw you in his last moments."

It infuriated Abby to know that with his last breath, Leo believed that she'd killed him. She didn't have much time to make amends for that. But first she had to handle the current problem. She couldn't release Margaret. The young vamp had tasted the power of taking a life and she'd liked it too well. There would be no stopping her now, and with her newly discovered gift of illusion no one was safe. No one. A young vampire's unstoppable hunger would bring the human world, Leo's world, on a hunt, and Abby would be at the center of it all. Even rogues practiced some restraint, some caution. Margaret would not.

Margaret was tough, and recently fed, and in the midst of finding her own powers. But she was not as old and strong as Abby. She seemed to finally remember that, as Abby raised her right hand and allowed the nails there to grow into five-inch razor sharp claws that curved upward.

Realizing what was about to happen, Margaret shimmered once more. To Abby's eyes it looked as if Leo stood before her, alive and mortal and beautiful. "He loved you, you know." Margaret's voice coming from Leo's mouth was wrong. "Until the end, when he thought you'd ended him, he loved you. He wasn't even sure why, the love was just there. Humans are silly that way, I suppose."

Abby ignored the face before her and remembered Margaret's form, and where Margaret's heart would be. With a cry that was loud in the night her blade-fingers sliced into Margaret's chest. So damaged, so violated, the young vampire could not maintain her illusion.

Abby grasped the dead heart within Margaret's chest and ripped it out.

Even though it did not beat, without the heart the vampire could not survive. Margaret looked at her own heart, she screamed, and then she and the heart turned to dust and a sudden night wind took it all.

Abby dropped to her knees beside Leo. His face was pale as death. It *was* death. He had not been dead long, there was time, but still, it was a risk. Only the strongest could survive being turned, and some were different after the change, as if who they had been inside did not survive. If the man she loved wasn't present in the monster she created, would she be able to end him as she'd ended Margaret?

With the nails she'd used to rip out Margaret's heart, Abby sliced a vein in her wrist. Blood dripped, and she quickly led that wrist to Leo's colorless lips. "Drink, love," she whispered. "There is life in my blood. Take it. Drink it. I swear, I don't want to live in a world without you in it."

Drops of blood hit his tongue, those drops seeped through his mouth, down the throat. After an agonizingly slow passage of minutes his heart beat once,

weakly. Only Abby could hear it. It beat again, and a
few minutes later again. His eyes snapped open and that
heartbeat stopped with a final thud.

For a moment he was terrified of the face above him,
and Abby understood why. For all Leo knew she had
been the one to kill him. But she watched as his expression changed. Terror, suspicion, confusion, then relief.
"Blonde," he said hoarsely. "Not you."

"Yes, dear," Abby said sweetly. "Blonde. Not me."

"You smell like cookies. She smelled like death."

"Cookies?"

He nodded weakly.

"Leo, darling, I want you to drink something."

"Drink what?" he asked, still ignorant to what was
happening, to what he had become.

"Me," she said, lying beside him and placing her
wrist against his mouth. "Drink of me."

Leo instinctively latched his mouth to her wrist and
suckled there. Gently at first, and then harder. He was
starving, and did not know how or why. A basic survival
instinct urged him on, forced him to drink long and
deep. They lay on the ground entangled, joined in a new
way. He took too much; she did not care, not even when
she passed out.

Abby had not slept in more than four hundred years;
she had not needed sleep. But then this was not sleep,
it was oblivion, a result of the loss of blood. Eventually, Leo slept, too, when he had drunk his fill. She
knew he slept because he joined her in her dream world.
They were together in her mind and soul, and in his.
They were linked. She would never again return to an

existence where she was alone. In her dream she clung
to him. Though she had only recently discovered the
depth of this bond, she knew that to be without it would
be worse than death.

Hours after she'd passed into oblivion with his
mouth at her wrist, she woke slowly to find Leo on top
of her. He kissed her healed wrist, licked her throat,
rubbed his body against hers. Already he had discovered a vampire's enhanced sensitivity, and a new urge
drove him. Without a word he pushed her skirt up,
over her hips. With insistent hands he spread her
thighs, he touched her intimately, his fingers dancing
on and inside her. He freed himself and filled her
quickly, thrusting inside her as if that connection was
as necessary for him as the blood with which she'd
given him life.

She came almost instantly, sending yet another cry
into the darkness of the night. Her body shook; she
trembled in an entirely human way, and yet she did not
think it a weakness. Leo's movements slowed. He was still
hard, still moving in and out of her in a fine, easy rhythm.

"Everything has changed," he whispered.

"Yes, love."

"I see, even though it is dark. I see you with a startling clarity, and you are more beautiful than you have
ever been. For a while I was gone, gone from everything, and then I woke with your scent in my nostrils
and when I touched you I found you warm. Not cold,
as you have been in the past, but warm."

"I will always be warm to you now."

"Yes. Nothing has ever felt so incredible, so right.

I'm inside you, you're inside me. I do not know where one of us ends and the other begins."

"We are one," she whispered, knowing it to be true. Beyond the physical joining of bodies, to the pit of their souls—if they had souls…

He moved faster, harder, and then he, too, came.

Leo lifted his head and looked down at her. He had already found his vampire eyes, and he saw her very well. "Abigail Smythe."

"You remember."

"I remember everything now. I see everything."

"I could not let you go," she whispered. Would he hate her? Would he hate what he had become when he understood fully how his life—his existence—had changed?

"I could never hate you," he said gently.

"You read my mind."

"Did I?"

A vampire who found his gift so quickly could only be a very powerful one. Then again, perhaps it was only her mind he could read, since they were so close. No, more than close, they were one being sharing two bodies. She had tasted his blood; he had tasted hers.

It was time to run again, to make a new home, to change her name, but this time…this time she wouldn't be running alone.

Leo paced Abby's apartment, still amazed at the vividness of the colors around him, still childlike in his wonder at all the sensations being a vampire afforded. Abby had him on pigs' blood for the time being, with an occasional nip of her blood, when the time was right.

She wasn't certain he could control himself with human blood in his mouth. Not yet. With his strength he would be unstoppable; even Abby couldn't best him, and she was pretty damn strong herself. She would teach him control, she said. The strength that had come with the change was incredible, and the sex was so good he was amazed he and Abby ever left their bed.

The case of Marisa's murder had been solved, though no one beyond the vampire community could ever know that justice had already been served. He'd presented the case to the ABI, along with a sharp gardening tool which would explain away the wounds at Marisa Blackwell's throat. A lot of people knew Remy had been seeing Marisa, and just as many people knew that Margaret was crazy jealous. A convenient statement from Abby's follower Charles indicating that he'd seen the two women together less than an hour before Marisa's death sealed the deal. A manhunt was on; they'd never find her, as there was nothing left to find.

He and Abby—and all the others, he assumed—would be leaving town, soon. He'd be able to explain away the fact that he only went to the station after dark for so long, before his coworkers started getting suspicious. Maybe there wasn't a Sherlock Holmes among them, but they weren't complete idiots, either.

Abby was still afraid, now and then, that he would hate her for turning him. He not only read her thoughts, he was washed in the emotions she claimed not to possess. Love and fear, guilt and joy, need and trepidation. Behind a stoic face she experienced them all, and he experienced them with her.

"We're going to be together forever," he said as he caught a snippet of a thought filled with doubt.

Though Abby's gift had never before allowed her to access a vampire mind, she was often able to see into his. Words and images, stray thoughts, every day that link grew stronger and clearer. When it was complete and eternal, as he suspected it soon would be, she'd have no more doubts.

She looked at him from across the room. When they were alone she didn't like clothes much, so she'd wrapped herself in that length of soft cloth that was sometimes draped across the back of her sofa. "You don't yet know what a very long time forever can be."

"Marry me."

She laughed in surprise. "Vampires don't get married!"

"Why not?"

"Because as I already said, forever is a *very long time*." She squared her shoulders. "Besides, can you imagine a bitter divorce between two immortals? It's best to just let a relationship run its course and then, when the time comes, move on."

He crossed the room to stand before her, looking her in the eye so she would have no doubts about what he had to say. "I love you. I'm not going anywhere. I suspect forever will not be long enough where you're concerned."

The strength that came with his new body was taking some getting used to, as was the speed. He actually had to make an effort not to move too quickly in the presence of humans, or to display his strength. But with Abby, he had to hide nothing. He picked her up now, as if she weighed nothing, and held her close as he very gently tasted her throat. The fabric she'd had wrapped around her body fell away. And in that moment, forever seemed very fine.

Epilogue

The Sundown Bar, located on a county road in northern Wisconsin, did a brisk business with hunters, vacationers and a handful of locals, especially on Friday and Saturday nights. During the week the human crowd was sparse, but the vamp crowd didn't change. Every one had followed Abby when she'd left Alabama. Where else were they going to get properly prepared pigs' blood and the company of their own kind? Where else could they get instruction from a powerful elder? The building had changed, the weather and the people had changed, but what went on inside the Sundown Bar had not changed much at all. Remy played piano, usually sticking to the jazz he loved. Abby waited tables. Leo tended bar. There was a small but very nice apartment on the second floor, where they made their home for now.

Outside, a thick December snow fell, blanketing the ground. The human customers often talked about Christmas coming. The presents, the food, the traveling. Over the river and through the woods…

To the locals the owners of the new bar were Abby and Leo Johnson. He'd wanted to choose a more exotic surname, but with the blasted Internet you couldn't be too careful. The more common the name, the better. In the interest of distancing themselves from what had once been, Leo had accepted that he was going to spend his life being a Johnson or a Smith or a Jones or a Brown. He really didn't care what anyone called him, as long as he had Abby beside him. If anyone ever got too close to the truth, they likely wouldn't even be able to keep their given names—in public, at least. A worry for another day.

The police chief in Budding Corner hadn't been too pleased when his newly hired detective left, running off with a local bartender in a flurry of scandal, and leaving the pursuit of one Margaret Harris—who would never be found—to others.

It had been a couple of months since they'd left Alabama, and there was still much to be done to tie up the loose ends. Leo called his family now and then, but he knew he couldn't ever see them again. If they saw his face they would know he was different. His eyes were a lighter shade of blue, his skin was smoother and paler. He looked slightly different; just enough that the people who knew him well would notice. Even if he could hide his strength and speed, those who knew him would be able to see that he moved differently. He could make his voice sound the way it once had, but he had to work at it. Yes, they would know he was not the Leo Stryker they knew and loved. A part of them would fear him, no matter how familiar he tried to appear.

One of these days he'd fake his death, he supposed. He hated to do that to his mother, but it was preferable to the truth—for her, at least. It had been hard enough telling her he wouldn't be home for Christmas this year. This Christmas, every holiday, every day of his existence to come, would be spent with Abby. Only Abby.

Abby's rules about munching on the customers still stood, and everyone knew it. No hunting within a ten-mile radius. But now and then the two of them made a trip to Milwaukee or Chicago and enjoyed a night on the town. Humans were weak-minded and easily swayed, he'd discovered, and damn, they tasted good. He and Abby could hook up with another couple, take a bit of blood—enough to sustain and gratify, but not enough to kill the donors—and then they'd leave the couple alone, with no memory that they'd ever met Abby and Leo Johnson or Smith or whatever.

Thanks to Abby he had never killed. Maybe he would, someday, if he had no other choice, as Abby had had no choice but to kill Margaret—a twisted vampire who had discovered joy in taking lives. He had enough human left in him to disdain the idea of unnecessarily taking a life. For now.

Now and then Abby asked him if he missed being human, but in truth there wasn't much to miss. Cherry pie, which now tasted like cardboard. Jack and Coke, which tasted like piss, these days. Cigarettes. He no longer had to worry about the health risks and they tasted like old socks. Didn't that just figure? Sunshine, which would instantly burn his skin like acid and would kill him if he stayed in the light long enough. Or so he'd been told. He hadn't worked up the nerve to test that particular lesson.

And yes, he did miss his family. They'd been a pain in the ass at times, but he had loved them. He loved them still, but they were better off not meeting the creature he'd become. In time, he wouldn't miss them at all, Abby told him. Already, his memories of them were fading. He knew who they were and he did care, but his memories of them were as if through murky, distorting glass.

Other than occasionally missing those things, which he could certainly live without, he was content. He passed his nights tending bar with Abby at his side, and his days in a thickly curtained suite of rooms decorated in shades of red and orange and the occasional hint of pink. They made love and read and danced. Naked. Abby was teaching him to paint. Maybe in a hundred years or so he'd be a decent enough artist, but he didn't think so.

Maybe he should take up the piano.

He'd discovered a new talent, since the change. Abby was surprised, but pleased, that he had found this new power so quickly. She considered it a sign of great strength, and great strength equaled survival. In the same way that she could see into the heads of humans when she so desired, he knew when they were telling the truth and when they were lying. Even something as simple as a "No, honey, that dress doesn't make you look fat" sent his radar pinging. Unlike Abby's gift, his was just as effective on vampires as it was on humans, though the signals themselves were different. A lie was a lie, no matter who told it. Abby thought it was hilarious, since he'd been a cop in the old days, that he was now a walking, talking lie detector.

He'd never caught her in a lie. He didn't expect he ever would.

It was a busy night, and Abby had her hands full with a table of thirsty hunters. While she took their order she looked at him and smiled.

Love you. She thought, and he heard the words as if she had spoken them, just for him.

Love you, too.

Remy played a lightning-fast version of "Take the A Train." The vampire customers put their heads together, whispering as they waited for humans to leave so they could claim *their* time and enjoy their late-night sustenance.

Leo didn't feel like a monster, though he knew there were those who would disagree, if they knew the truth. As long as he could love, he wouldn't feel like a monster in the truest sense. As long as Abby loved him, she was much more than the stuff of nightmares. Together they were better than they had ever been apart, no matter what the cost.

One of these days, she was going to marry him. She'd come around. As she said, forever was a long time.

Abby walked to the bar with the hunters' orders in hand. With a nod of her head she signaled to Charles, who'd been filling in now and then and doing a decent enough job. Leo tossed his bar towel down and followed Abby toward the door, in sync with her, following her lead without conscious thought. As she opened the front door one of the hunters called out, "You two better grab your coats! It's cold out there!"

Abby smiled at him. "We won't be long." Then she closed the door behind her, and hand in hand, they walked out into the parking lot, into the snow. Leo lifted the hand Abby did not hold and let a few snowflakes land there. "It's not cold at all. Feels like a whisper of rain, only lighter. A mist off the water, maybe."

"Close your eyes."

He did.

"Feel the fall of snow on your face."

He did.

"It's a little like sunshine," Abby said. "If you use your imagination, you can almost feel as if you're standing on the beach on a summer's day."

She had often asked him if he missed human things, but he had never asked the same of her. He did now, as they stood in the snow and imagined another place and time.

"There have been moments," she said, after a short, thoughtful pause. "I used to occasionally miss apples, and the sun on my face, and even the release of shedding tears. There have been times when I missed the beat of my own heart, and good dreams and the feel of waking up in the morning and stretching out sleepy muscles." She looked up at him and her mind joined with his.

But I don't miss anything any longer, because now

I have you and I can ask for nothing more from this existence. Kiss me, Leo, kiss me in the falling snow.
  He did.

* * * * *

Don't miss Linda Winstead Jones's next Nocturne
LAST OF THE RAVENS
Coming January 2010

NOTHING SAYS CHRISTMAS LIKE A VAMPIRE

Lisa Childs

Dear Reader,

I am thrilled to be included in the
Holiday with a Vampire III anthology!

This is such a hectic time of year that it's
important to be able to take a break from all the
shopping and baking and, here in Michigan,
snow-shoveling. The way that I take a break is to
lose myself in a really good story. I hope you'll
find "Nothing Says Christmas Like a Vampire" to
be a compelling read.

Sienna Briggs is having a horrible holiday as she
has to say goodbye to her beloved grandmother.
But then she meets a handsome, mysterious
stranger who introduces her to a world she'd be
safer not knowing about…because the Secret
Vampire Society is a secret mortals can't learn
about and still live. Julian Vossimer wants to
protect Sienna, but he winds up putting her in
more danger. Fortunately the holidays are a time
for miracles and for stories of love that defy all
odds.

Happy holidays and happy reading!

Lisa Childs

Chapter 1

Sienna Briggs stood alone beside her grandmother's casket. Twinkling lights, wound around pine boughs, reflected back from the shiny surface. Her hands trembled against the lid as she closed it, hiding her grandmother's beautiful face. "Goodbye," she whispered into the silence, the funeral home empty but for her. "Tell Gramps Merry Christmas."

The elderly couple had loved the holidays, and each other, so much. They would be so happy to be together again. Sienna blinked back tears, refusing to feel sorry for herself over being alone. Nana had made Sienna promise to celebrate Christmas. Of course, at the end, her grandmother had said a lot of things that hadn't made much sense. Had to have been the drugs talking....

Maybe the painkillers had been the reason she'd insisted Sienna keep the ring. She stared down at her right hand, and the finger onto which Nana had slid her engagement ring the day that she had died. The diamond twinkled more brightly than the Christmas lights. Sienna had wanted to bury it with Nana, but the older woman had been adamant that Sienna wear it—on her right hand until she met the man who would slide it onto her left hand.

"You will meet him," Nana had promised. "You'll meet the man who loves you with all his heart."

"Yeah, right…" The last thing Sienna expected to find under her tree this Christmas was a man. A pile of bills, an eviction notice, probably, but not a man. Chuckling to herself over Nana's romantic notions, she turned away from the casket, and collided with a tall, hard figure. Her hands trembled as she lifted them to his chest to brace herself. The heat of his body penetrated his black silk shirt, warming her palms and making her skin tingle.

He lifted his hands to cup her shoulders. His deep voice was a low rumble as he warned her, "Careful…"

"I thought everyone had left," she said. Even the funeral director had gone, with instructions to pull the door shut behind her and it would lock. The holidays were fast approaching, so he had probably wanted to get home to his family.

So this strange man wasn't an employee of the mortician, and he was too young to have been a friend of Nana's. Yet something about him was eerily familiar. The deep-set dark eyes, the finely chiseled features and the black hair that hung just past his broad shoulders—all of it struck a chord in her memory. Especially the small diamond-shaped scar near the cleft in his chin.

Her heart hammered against her ribs, and fear cracked her voice as she asked, "Who are you?"

"I think you know," he challenged her.

Beneath her palm, his heart pounded hard. Realizing she still touched him, she curled her fingers and pulled away her hands.

"I'm sorry." She shook her head, her mind muddled with confusion and exhaustion—and his distracting nearness. "I don't know you."

But a thought, buried in the dark recesses of her mind, tugged at her. Sienna refused to recall the dark memories though; monsters lurked with those memories, threatening to hurt her. Again. That was why, even at twenty-seven, she still slept with the lights on.

He didn't release her, his fingers holding tight to her shoulders. "Don't be sorry," he said as if it didn't matter, yet something about his tone suggested that it did. "It was a long time ago."

She jerked from his grasp, suddenly very aware that they were all alone…except for the dead. "Don't pretend to know me when you don't."

"Sienna…"

She shivered. He knew *her* name. But he could have learned it from reading her grandmother's obituary. "Who are you?" she asked again. "Or should I ask *what* are you?"

He sucked in a ragged breath. "What do you mean?"

"I know you're a con man."

A muscle twitched just above the line of his tightly clenched jaw as anger and pride flashed through his dark eyes. "Sienna—"

"Don't waste your time with me," she advised him, "I have nothing for you to con me out of." Only the ring.

He caught her hand in his, but instead of reaching for the diamond, he wrapped his fingers around her wrist where her pulse leaped with a rush of heat and adrenaline from his touch. "I am not a *con* man."

"I don't expect you to admit that you are," she said with a short laugh. "You won't even tell me your name and how you know me."

"I don't have time to explain," he said with a glance over his shoulder.

Sienna couldn't see what he was looking at; he was so much taller than her, his shoulders so broad, that she could see nothing but him—his handsome face, his muscular chest straining the buttons of his silk shirt. Over the shirt and jeans, he wore a long wool jacket—open, as if the cold outside didn't affect him at all.

"You're going to have to trust me." He stroked his thumb across the leaping pulse point in her wrist.

She swallowed hard, but her throat remained dry with nerves and a sudden rush of desire. How could she be attracted to a man she just met and who frightened her so much?

In protest of her attraction as much as his command, she murmured, "No…" She tried to tug free of him again, but he held her with his dark-eyed gaze and his grasp.

Then he pulled her closer so that her breasts pushed

against the hard wall of his chest. "Once I get you out of here, I will tell you everything."

She shook her head, trying to break the connection between them. "I'm not going anywhere with you. Let me go!"

He tightened his hold and slid an arm around her back, so she couldn't escape him. "I can't. I came here for you, Sienna. I'm going to save you."

I'm going to save you...

The words reverberated inside her mind. And she flashed back to big hands reaching out of the darkness for her, pulling her from the twisted metal that was all that was left of her parents' vehicle. Staring deep into those compelling dark eyes of his, she remembered now where she had seen him before—when she was seven and had become an orphan.

She grimaced as the old memories pummeled her; the screech of metal as the car struck the guardrail, sparks flying. Then the crunch as the rail broke, and the car tumbled down the hillside, end over end. The screaming—her mother's screams and hers...echoed inside her head.

She shook her head, trying to wake herself from the nightmare. The pain, the fear, the darkness...it was all too much. She clutched at him, pleading, "Make it stop..."

He leaned forward, his mouth nearing hers as if he intended to kiss her. But before his lips touched hers, it stopped. *Everything* stopped.

Julian Vossimer caught her, as her body went limp against his, and he lifted her in his arms, holding her close to his madly pounding heart. Her head settled into the crook of his shoulder and neck, her breath warm and whisper-soft against his skin.

His blood pounded in his veins, not just over the imminent danger she was in—but because of the danger she had put him in. The danger of falling for her.

She had become such a beautiful woman. Her hair, the same honey-tone as her skin, bore shimmery streaks of sunshine. Her eyes, although closed now, were a bright blue that had glistened with the tears she'd fought as she told her grandmother goodbye. Those tears had been the only hint of her grief, of mourning. The visitation room for her grandmother was decorated with red and white poinsettias, lights, pine boughs and a Christmas tree. Instead of traditional black, Sienna wore a red dress in soft velvet that hugged every curve of her tempting body. But he didn't intend to seduce her; his only intention was to protect her. Yet had he actually hurt her? Or had she fainted just from fear?

If she was this afraid now, what would she be when she learned what he really was?

"She's fine," he assured himself. For now. But if he couldn't get her to listen to him, she wouldn't be fine. She would be as dead as her grandmother.

Balancing her slight body in one arm, he grabbed up her purse and jacket from a chair in front of the casket. He found her keys then draped her coat over her before slipping out a back door to the parking lot. He couldn't have witnesses who could identify him as the man with whom Sienna Briggs had disappeared.

And she had to disappear, in order to save her life.

Her breath escaped in white puffs into the night air, and snow drifted down, falling in wispy flakes onto her beautiful face. The flakes melted and slid down her skin like tears. He suspected she had shed a lot of tears in her life. She had lost so many people she loved.

Because of Julian. Guilt twisted his gut. If only…

But he could not change the past. He could only affect the future. And he had to make sure she had one. He wouldn't be responsible for taking that away from her, too.

Julian pushed the button on her keys, so that the lights on a small SUV flashed on and off while the locks opened with an audible click. He had to take her car, too, so no one would realize from where she'd gone missing. But would anyone realize she was missing?

Few people had showed up tonight to pay their re- spects to her grandmother, or offer their support to Sienna. She seemed so alone now, as if she had less than when he'd pulled her from that wreckage almost twenty years ago. Regret joined his guilt.

"I'm sorry…" he murmured as he pulled open the passenger's door and settled her limp body onto the seat.

He should have warmed up the car; her skin chilled, the snowflakes no longer melted on her face, but clung to her lashes. Suddenly light flashed, momentarily blinding Julian as fire sprang up around the vehicle. He hadn't moved fast enough to protect her.

"No!" he shouted. "Leave her alone!" But he didn't want her alone, he wanted her with him.

A woman stepped out of the smoke, her eyes burning as brightly as the flames—with hatred and madness. "Vossimer, step back…"

Ignoring her order, Julian reached through the flames and gathered Sienna back into his arms. Clutching her close, he wrapped his coat around them both. "I'm not going to let you kill her…"

"She has to die," Ingrid Montgomery argued. "I was there. I heard her grandmother tell her the secret."

"The woman was terminally ill." As Ingrid knew since she had posed as a hospice nurse. "Sienna won't believe what she heard."

"If she'd seen this, she would." Ingrid pulled a picture from the pocket of her cloak. Across the space separating them, Julian recognized a young version of Sienna's grandmother and himself. "She'd realize you aren't human."

"You don't know that," he insisted. "Burn the picture, not her. She won't repeat what her grandmother said."

"Like her grandmother wouldn't repeat the secret? You can't trust humans," the woman said, the pitch of her voice rising to the level of a hysterical scream. "You can't trust them. You know what happens…"

Not as painfully as she knew. "Ingrid—"

"If we don't kill her," the woman persisted, "more of *us* will die."

Julian shook his head. "She's already suffered enough. I won't hurt her."

"I figured you were too attached to her," Ingrid said, "so I brought reinforcements."

Her *reinforcements* stepped from the shadows, but the darkness remained part of them, buried deep in whatever was left of their souls. He glanced at the three men, all big and burly and more than willing to do Ingrid's bidding.

Anger coursed through him, vibrating in his voice as he shouted, "Stay back!"

"Let her go and you won't get hurt," Ingrid negotiated. "I'll clean up your mess for you."

"She's not my mess—"

"She's too much to you," Ingrid said with a snort of disgust, "and she's too dangerous for the rest of us. You know the rule—no human can learn the secret of our existence and live. She must die, Julian. Now."

"She's not a threat—" he turned to the men who inched closer to him "—to any one of us."

"That's not what your grandfather says—that's not what he sees," Ingrid reminded him.

Julian's heart clenched with dread. "My grandfather…" That was why Ingrid had posed as the hospice worker, to make sure Carolina Briggs died. Orson Vossimer had threatened to order her death long ago—not because of what he suspected but hadn't been able to prove she knew—but to reclaim their family honor. "He's behind all of this?"

Julian wasn't surprised; he was *sickened*. How long could the old man hold a grudge?

"Your grandfather's worried about you," Ingrid said. "He believes you've lost your objectivity, that your pity for the little girl she once was has clouded your judgment. All grown-up, she is a threat to you, but you can't see it."

He could see—and feel—that Sienna Briggs was all grown-up now. But a threat? Probably. He would admit that only to himself, though. He shook his head again. "I'm not going to let you kill her."

Ingrid's reinforcements eased closer to him and the flames that still lapped around the burning vehicle.

"You're going to have to kill me first," Julian threatened, "and I don't think that would make my *grandfather* very happy."

Ingrid gasped, as if shocked by his ultimatum, and her men halted their approach, uncertain how to proceed.

Julian took advantage of their indecision. Clutching Sienna more tightly in his arms, he leaped and launched them into the sky. The falling snow, cold and hard, struck his face as he propelled them higher.

The flames rose, licking at the sky and nipping at Julian's heels. But he flew, cutting through the thick black air. Even though the reinforcements, spurred on by Ingrid's shouts, chased him, he was too fast and too motivated. He outdistanced them with ease until not even a wisp of smoke reached him.

Sienna shifted in his arms and murmured, as if she was regaining consciousness. She had already been out so long. Perhaps exhaustion, more than fear, had caused her to collapse. He tightened his grip, so that she wouldn't slip from his hold. He had to get her to safety—had to return her to land before she awakened. She had been frightened of him *before*—he couldn't risk her awakening during flight. If she fought him...

If she fell...

Instead of saving her, he might wind up being the one responsible for her death...as he was responsible for other deaths.

Chapter 2

Sienna's eyes opened—to total blackness. Panic pressed against her chest, and a scream burned in her throat, escaping in a mere gasp of breath.

"Shh," a deep voice murmured. "You're all right. Everything's fine." Flames flickered as he lit candles. The soft light illuminated the room.

The bedroom. Sienna lay on a soft mattress, a brown suede bedspread pulled to her chin. The drapes, drawn across the windows, were also brown and so thick that they blocked any hint of moonlight or streetlamps. The candlelight didn't dispel her panic as her fear increased. "Wh-where am I? Where did you take me?"

"Home."

She glanced around at the plaster walls that stretched

ten feet to a coffered ceiling. An ornate chandelier hung from the center, but only the reflection of the candle-light shimmered in the crystal and leaded glass.

She shook her head. "This isn't my home."

"This is *my* home."

"Your bed?"

He nodded, his black hair skimming across his broad shoulders. He'd ditched his jacket and wore only the black silk shirt now, pulled free of the waist of his dark pants. Several shirt buttons had been opened, revealing the sculpted muscles of his chest.

Sienna shivered.

"You're still cold?"

Her fingers trembling, she lifted the blanket and peered beneath. She still wore her clothes, but the red velvet dress had twisted, the hem tangled around her hips. "You—you didn't undress me…"

"Did you want me to?" he asked as he settled onto the bed next to her, his hip pressed against hers.

"I— Of course not," she replied. And she tried to shift away, but he stretched his arm across her and planted his palm atop the blanket on the other side of her, trapping her in the bed—her face just inches from his. She tried to ignore his closeness and tried not to stammer as she demanded, "I want to know why—how—when you brought me here."

He opened his mouth, as if he intended to answer at least one of those questions. But Sienna needed to know something else first, so she put a finger across his lips. "Who the hell are you?"

"My name is Julian Vossimer."

The name meant nothing to her. But the man did—if he really was the one she remembered from that old nightmare. Yet everyone had told her that that had been just a dream, her mind playing tricks on her...like Nana's had been playing tricks on her at the end.

"I don't understand," she said, "why I'm here."

"We need to talk, Sienna," he said, his deep voice lowered to a soft whisper. "I have some things to tell you, some things you need to hear."

"I remember."

"What?" He tensed. "*What* do you remember?"

The memories didn't surge back like they had, violently, at the funeral home. They were just *there* now—like she was just *here* with him. It hadn't been a dream or a trick of her mind, no matter what anyone had tried to convince her.

"I remember that night," she said, "that you were the one who pulled me from the wreckage." He hadn't just pulled her, though. He'd had to manipulate the twisted metal, wrenching it apart before he'd been able to get her free. Maybe she had dreamed that part because no man was capable of such strength. Since he had saved her once, she shouldn't fear him now. "I guess I owe you...my life..."

A muscle flinched in the deep crease of his lean cheek. His face was all sculpted planes and hard lines that tempted her finger to trace and touch. Did it matter what else he was, or why he'd brought her here?

"You're my hero..."

The muscle jerked again as he shook his head. "I'm no hero."

"Did you bring me here to hurt me?" she asked, but she already knew that he hadn't. If she'd felt she was in real danger from him, she would have started fighting to escape him. It wouldn't make sense for him to have saved her all those years ago to hurt her now.

"No," he answered her, his dark eyes serious and sincere. "I brought you here to protect you."

"See, you're my hero," she said. Maybe it was his eyes—those deep-set dark eyes that pulled her into his soul. Maybe it was the attraction, quivering inside her, that she'd never felt as intensely for another man. But she leaned forward and lifted her face to his. Her lips skimmed across that diamond-shaped scar on his chin before she kissed him.

His mouth moved against hers as he took possession of her. His lips parted hers, and his tongue slipped inside, tasting her. He eased her back onto the pillow and followed her down.

Sienna had never been kissed as thoroughly. She slid her hands into his hair, tangling her fingers in the silky black strands as she clutched his nape. But he pulled away, breathing so heavily that his chest pushed against her breasts.

"I'm not cold anymore," she murmured. But then reality intruded, reminding her that she didn't know this man. Not really. She had only a child's exaggerated memory of the man who'd saved her life. This same man, who appeared not even a day older, although nearly twenty years had passed. She shivered again.

"You're not?"

"I'm scared," she admitted. Scared of the feelings he

drew out of her—feelings she'd promised herself she would never risk experiencing. She'd already lost too many people she cared about; it was easier to stop caring.

He said nothing, just continued to stare at her with that molten dark gaze.

"This is where you're supposed to tell me that I have nothing to fear," she prodded him.

"I can't."

"No, because then you wouldn't need to protect me." She reached up and traced the line of his jaw to the scar on his chin. "Why do you need to protect me?"

Did he know about the mounting debts? Did he pity her for having no one and nothing left?

He stared down at her, his conflict apparent in his dark eyes. "I thought I needed to protect you from… from something else…but now I think I need to protect you from me."

A smile twitched at her lips. "I don't need protecting from anyone," she assured him. "I can take care of myself. I've been taking care of myself for a long while." Except for that night, when he'd pulled her from the twisted metal of what had once been the family sedan.

"For a long while, you've been taking care of everyone else," he said. "Your grandfather. Your grandmother."

How did he know so much about her? How did he know that she had cared for both her grandparents through long illnesses? Both had died from cancer. "Have you been watching me?"

All these years…

"I know you," he claimed, "I know that you haven't taken care of yourself."

"I said that I had— That I can…"

He shook his head. "You were so focused on your family that you didn't take care of yourself. I don't think you know how."

"Of course I know how."

"When have you ever done something for yourself?" he asked. "Something just for you?"

She slid her fingers back into his hair. "This. You. This is the first time in…" Forever that she remembered thinking only of herself, thinking only of her pleasure. Not her pain. And she had no idea why. Remembering who he was had brought all that pain crashing back, the force of it so strong that it had rendered her unconscious. But now, in his bed, in his arms, desire held that pain at bay.

She knew it would come crashing back again with the reality of all that she had lost and with how alone she was. But in his bed, in his arms, she wasn't alone. And she wanted that feeling to last. She wanted nothing to do with reality for the rest of the night.

She pulled his head down to hers and kissed him with all the passion burning inside her. His mouth opened as he sighed her name, and Sienna slid her tongue across his bottom lip. And across the line of his teeth which was even but for the point—the sharp point of an incisor. Yet it was longer than a mere incisor and sharper.

Like a fang.

And she realized why he had not aged a day since he'd rescued her. The man was immortal. The man was not a man. *He was a vampire.*

* * *

She knew.

The minute her tongue had brushed across the tip, his fang had distended. Usually he could control it— usually he could control his passion. But not with her.

Not with Sienna kissing him, her fingers running through his hair, clutching at it to hold his mouth to hers. But then she pulled back and shoved her trembling hands against his chest, pushing him away.

Her eyes, wide with horror, stared up at him, and she stammered, "You're— You're a…"

She couldn't speak the word aloud, but then neither could he, for so many reasons.

"Sienna, you're upset—exhausted. You're not thinking clearly," he tried to convince her. "You need to rest."

"I need to leave," she said, her voice steady now and her hands stronger as she pushed at his chest.

He wouldn't budge, refusing to ease up. Instead he lowered his body more heavily onto hers, holding her down. She wriggled beneath him, her hips grinding against his erection as her breasts pushed against his chest. He groaned and closed his eyes until she stilled. Her breath, ragged with fear and exertion, blew hot against his throat.

"Let me go," she pleaded.

He shook his head. "I can't let you go."

"Yes, you can," she implored, "you saved me once. No one else would have found the car. I would have died—if you hadn't come along when you had…"

Guilt wound around his heart, clenching it. He'd seen the car crash, but light had been breaking through the night sky, the sun rising. And he hadn't been able to get to her then—not without risking his own life. He'd had to wait until darkness fell again. He'd had to leave her alone, for hours, with her dead parents—scared, possibly hurt. He would never forgive himself. And if she knew, neither would she.

"I'm saving you now," he insisted, "by keeping you here. If I let you go, you won't survive." As she had survived all those hours alone in the tangled car wreck. She was in infinitely more danger now than she'd been then.

"I told you I can take care of myself," she reminded him. "I don't need you…"

He was afraid that he needed *her;* his body ached and throbbed with desire for her. A desire more powerful than he'd ever felt before…for *any* other woman.

Her slender throat moved as she swallowed and added, "…to protect me."

"You have no idea of the danger you're in."

She stared up at him, fear still widening her eyes. "I think I do…"

"You can trust me. I would never hurt you." Intentionally. But inadvertently he already had. He lifted his hand to her face, cupping her cheek in his palm. Then he skimmed his thumb along the curve of her delicate jaw. Her skin was so silky. He lowered his head, his lips just brushing her throat as he breathed deeply, inhaling the sweet scent of vanilla and the sweeter scent of her blood.

Hunger burned inside him, hunger to taste her.

She shuddered, as if able to read his mind. And maybe she could. Her grandmother had certainly had that gift. She'd known things he hadn't told her, things he hadn't admitted even to himself. He hadn't loved her; he'd only wanted her for her beauty. She'd been right to deny him. Sienna was even more beautiful than her grandmother and probably just as smart if not smarter. No doubt she would deny him, too.

"I won't hurt you," he said again, as he stared into her eyes, willing her to believe him. Willing her to trust him even though he wasn't entirely certain he could trust himself—with her.

Her eyes dilated, the pupils eclipsing the glittery blue. "This seems like a dream," she murmured. "I must be just dreaming…"

"What do you dream of?" he wondered.

"You…" Her breath caught, quivering in her chest. "I dream of arms reaching out, pulling me to safety, holding me close. I dream of *you*…"

"Sienna…" He didn't deserve the gratitude he glimpsed in her eyes. He was no hero.

"I didn't think you were real," she admitted. "Everyone told me that I must have made you up, but they had no explanation for how I'd gotten free. No human could have twisted apart that metal. But nobody was around when they found me by the side of the road. So I began to believe them, to believe that I'd only imagined you." She lifted her hands to his face, her fingers trembling as she traced his jaw. "But here you are, and I'm still not sure you're real."

"I'm real…" And desire had driven him beyond his guilt and regrets. He caught her hands in his and turned his face, nuzzling her wrist. Her pulse leaped beneath his lips, racing.

"But you're a…" She shook her head. "I didn't think Nana was lucid when she told me about…" She swallowed hard, the creamy skin of her throat rippling. "I thought it had just been the drugs making her talk crazy…"

So Ingrid hadn't been lying. Sienna knew… *things*…no mortal could know and live.

"Hell," she scoffed, "maybe I'm the one who's crazy. Before I woke up—here—I had the strangest sensation as if I was flying…" She released a shaky sigh. "Or floating…"

"You're not crazy, Sienna," he assured her. But *he* was for thinking he could save her. Because now, knowing for certain that she'd learned about the Underground Society, there was only one way he could do that…

"Yes, I am," she insisted, "because even knowing what you are, I want…" She pressed her lips together and closed her eyes, as if willing the words back, or herself somewhere else.

"What, Sienna?" he asked, his heart pounding hard and fast. Maybe he wasn't so crazy after all. "What do you want?"

She opened her eyes, and along with her fear, he glimpsed the fascination. And desire?

Her voice whisper-soft, she admitted, *"You."*

Chapter 3

Passion burned in his eyes—brighter than the flickering candles. And Sienna wished she could take back her admission, scared of his reaction and hers. This…man…had some kind of unnatural hold on her. His dark gaze drew her in, hypnotizing her into forgetting what he was…and the danger he posed to her.

She shook her head, her hair rustling against the satin pillowcase. "I didn't mean it…"

"You didn't mean to *say* it," he astutely surmised. "But you meant it. I can see it in your eyes, in the flush on your skin. You want *me*."

Even knowing it was too late, that she was in too deep, she shook her head again and hotly denied, "No!"

"Liar," he accused, his low voice vibrating with a sexy chuckle.

Julian Vossimer with his long, silky hair and hard muscled body epitomized *sexy*. And Sienna was powerless to resist her attraction to him. As he had accused her earlier, it had been a long time—too long for her to remember—the last time she'd done something just for herself. But making love to him…

Did she dare?

Taking the choice from her, he rolled off her and left the bed. She must have imagined the passion in his eyes. While she wanted him, he didn't want her.

Standing beside the bed, he stared down at her—his dark eyes still aglow. And his fingers went to the buttons on his shirt. First he undid the cuffs then the rest of the buttons down the front, parting the silk to reveal the sculpted muscles of his chest.

Sienna swallowed. His masculine beauty as the candlelight bathed his skin made her lose her breath. She found her voice, although raspy and weak, to ask, "What are you doing?"

His lips curved into a slight, wicked grin, and he reached for his belt, unclasping and pulling it free of his dark jeans. "I'm coming to bed…"

Then the jeans, and his boxers along with them, dropped to the floor. And Sienna's jaw dropped, too. Her mouth fell open and she gasped. His erection jutted from lean hips and heavily muscled thighs—so thick and long. When once she'd been so cold, now her skin heated—burning—but before she could push back the blanket, he jerked it off her.

He reached for her next, his hands shaking slightly, as he wrapped them around her upper arms and lifted her to her knees on the soft mattress. "Try to tell me you don't want me now," he challenged her.

The lie caught in her throat, choked with desire. She couldn't…resist him. She slid her hands over his chest, and his heart pounded against her palm—in perfect rhythm with the frantic beat of hers.

"You're so arrogant," she admonished him. But not without damn good reason.

Could any woman resist him?

The glow dimmed in his eyes for a moment, as if he'd taken insult at her comment.

"I'm sorry," she murmured.

"You're not the one who has cause to be sorry," he told her.

Not yet. But would she if they made love? Would she live to regret what she'd done? Would she live at all?

He must have glimpsed the fear in her eyes, for he stroked his thumb along her jaw again. "Don't be afraid," he said, "I won't hurt you."

She already hurt, aching for his touch—for his kiss. For the possession of his body. She stared into his handsome face, mesmerized by his dark gaze. "Julian…"

He leaned over her, lowering his mouth until just a breath separated their lips. "Do you want me?" he asked.

She slid her hands up his chest, muscles rippling beneath her palms, and tunneled her fingers through his thick, silky hair to grasp his nape. "You know I do…" She pulled his head down so that their lips met.

The kiss was feather-soft and nearly innocent. Then

she opened her mouth, and his tongue slid across her lower lip, stroking the sensitive flesh before dipping inside to taste her. Innocence fled as he made love to her mouth, his tongue driving in and out, sliding over hers.

His fingers knotted in the fabric of her dress. Then he dragged it up—their lips parting as he pulled the velvet over her head then dropped it to the floor. His breath shuddered out as his gaze traveled over her body, over the bits of scarlet lace covering her breasts and the curve of her hips.

"You're beautiful," he praised, the words a raspy groan of appreciation. "So beautiful…"

It wasn't the first time she'd been told, but it was the first time a compliment had affected her so that her nipples hardened, pushing against the thin lace, and heat rushed through her, burning between her thighs. She swallowed down a whimper that tickled the back of her throat.

But then he touched her, with just his fingertips, gliding them over her shoulders, along the ridge of her collarbone to the curve of her breasts. And the whimper slipped free even before those clever fingers reached the aching points of her nipples. When he touched them, sliding his fingers back and forth over the lace, she moaned and arched her neck.

Fear flickered to life. What if he took that gesture as an invitation to bite her?

"I won't hurt you," he repeated, his voice raspy with passion, as if he'd read her mind. His hands moved, sliding around her back to the clasp of her bra, which he undid. Then he pushed the straps down her arms so that the bit of lace fell away—leaving her breasts naked to his touch.

He cupped the mounds. And he kissed her lips again, deeply, as he gently massaged her sensitive flesh. Her nipples pushed against his palms, and she arched again—needing more from him than kisses.

His mouth broke from hers, and she panted for breath as his lips slid down her throat, his tongue flicking over her leaping pulse before moving lower. He traced the curve of each breast before closing his lips around one aching point. His tongue flicked across the sensitive tip.

She cried out and shuddered, a mini-orgasm rippling through her, dampening her panties. "Julian," she panted his name now, aching for more pleasure. Her hands moved, sliding down the rippling muscles of his back to the curve of his buttocks. She raked her nails over the taut skin. And now she pleaded, "Julian…"

He shook his head, his lips tugging at her nipple. Then he lifted his head. "Not yet…"

"Now," she begged, "please…"

He pushed her back then knelt on the mattress, between her legs. His hand shaking slightly, he tore the lace from her hips then lifted her thighs to his shoulders. He skimmed his mouth along the sensitive skin of her inner thighs, making her quiver, before kissing her intimately. His tongue stroked over her cleft before slipping inside and tasting. A moan of pleasure slipped from his throat.

Tears stung Sienna's eyes at the exquisite torture. Pressure built inside her, more intense and painful than she'd ever experienced. "You're hurting me," she murmured. "I'm hurting…"

But his fangs only pressed lightly against her swollen mound as his tongue dipped deeper inside her. His hands moved—one to a breast, which he molded, the other to the most sensitive part of her. His thumb pushed against the nub, breaking the pressure free inside her as an orgasm slammed through her.

She screamed, the pleasure tearing her apart. But then he moved, his mouth sliding over her navel, up her ribs to the tip of a breast. His lips tugged at the nipple as the tip of his erection pushed through her wet curls.

She wrapped her legs around his lean waist, her fingers sliding down to his butt again to clutch him to her. She stretched, trying to accept him, as the pressure built again. He was so big—so thick—that her skin burned. Then he slid so deep, he touched her where she'd never been touched. Pleasure exploded, so intense, that she fought to retain consciousness. "Julian!"

"Sienna!" he shouted her name, as if he, too, were shocked by the power of their passion. He thrust, driving deeper and deeper.

She clung to him, matching his frantic rhythm. The pressure wound tight inside her then exploded again, shattering her as she came even more powerfully than before.

He tensed, every muscle rippling, his skin slick with passion. He threw back his head, the tendons in his neck jutting out, as he uttered a guttural groan. Then he pumped his orgasm inside her, filling her as he came. His body shuddered, as finally spent, he clutched her in his arms and rolled to his side.

Sienna stroked her hands across his broad shoulders and through his hair, as if trying to soothe him, even as her own heart beat madly from an exertion that was not just physical. What the hell was she doing? Had she not only made love with a vampire, but fallen in love with him, too?

"Julian…"

The voice called to him out of the darkness. Not Sienna's voice. She slept in his arms, her head on his chest—almost as if she trusted him. But he didn't deserve her trust.

"Julian!" Impatience sharpened the masculine tone. And he recognized his telepathic *caller*.

"Grandfather," he answered the summons, speaking the words only inside his head.

"You foolish boy," Orson Vossimer berated him. "You think you can hide her from me?"

Boy. No matter the centuries Julian had existed, to his grandfather he would always be a boy. Never a man.

"You don't know where we are," he called the old man's bluff. He'd been careful to let no thought of their whereabouts pass through his mind—the mind his grandfather had always been too easily able to read.

"I will," Orson vowed. "Soon. You better fix this before we find you. I'm tired of cleaning up your messes, boy."

Julian winced. "You're overreacting. Just like before…"

"And just like before, you're too arrogant," his grandfather reprimanded him, "and too careless. You're not just endangering yourself, but everyone else in the Underground Society."

"She's no threat and you know it," Julian challenged him. "Just like her grandmother was no threat."

"And her father?"

Julian sucked in a breath. "You didn't need to—"

"Save the Underground from an inevitable massacre?"

"You nearly killed a little girl," Julian said, his arms contracting around Sienna's sleeping body. His fingers tunneled through her silky blond tresses.

"If she had died, it would have saved you from making another mess," Orson said with none of the regret and guilt that haunted Julian. "Like you're making now."

"She's not a mess."

"You're the mess, boy," Orson said, "and I can't keep bailing you out. You're a liability the Underground can't afford."

"None of this is about the Underground," Julian surmised. "This is about the Vossimer name."

"You've dishonored the family," Orson admitted. "And by hiding her away, you've done nothing to restore the honor."

"So I'm a liability to the Vossimers, as well as the Underground?"

"A liability neither can afford."

Julian shuddered. He'd always known the old man barely tolerated him. But hate him? "Are you threatening me?"

"I'm cautioning you to do the right thing."

"Your definition of right and mine are completely different."

"We've been at odds for years," Orson admitted. "That's your problem. You won't listen. Maybe it's time you stop being a problem."

Julian had no doubt now. Not only would Sienna lose her life if they were discovered, he would lose his, too. There was no changing his grandfather's mind.

"You have one option, Julian."

Orson Vossimer giving him an escape? "So what is this option?"

"*You* have to kill her."

"That's not an option. As long as I live, Sienna won't die," he vowed.

"Then make her one of us," Orson advised. "One of the undead."

"It's not that easy." To make her undead, she would have to risk death. She would have to trust him completely, and he'd never turned a human before. Even though he'd already determined it was his only way to save her, he didn't trust himself to not accidentally kill her. And if he couldn't trust himself, he couldn't expect her to trust him, either.

"It's quite simple, son," Orson insisted. "Turn her or you'll both die."

"She still may die," Julian pointed out. And he'd be the one who'd personally killed her. Was that what his grandfather counted on?

He received no reply. Orson had severed their telepathic connection. And Julian would have to work to block his grandfather's return to his mind. He couldn't be found yet—not until he had time to earn Sienna's trust. His heart clenched as he admitted to himself he wanted more than her trust. He wanted her love.

He muffled a snort of self-derision. He was the fool his grandfather thought him if he actually believed he could earn anyone's love. His own parents hadn't wanted him and Orson had only taken him out of family obligation and honor. And while many women had wanted Julian over the centuries he'd lived, none of them had actually loved him—not enough to want to spend eternity with him.

He focused on Sienna, studying her beautiful face as she slept. She turned, arching her neck against the pillow. He leaned forward and nuzzled the delicate skin of her throat, breathing in the sweet fragrance that was her very spirit.

If he were smart, he would forget about her trust and her love, and he'd take her now. He'd take the choice away from her and turn her into what he was. Undead. But if he failed, she'd die….

Chapter 4

A scream burned Sienna's throat when she opened her eyes to blackness. As memories rushed back, panic pressed down on her chest, making it hard for her to breathe. She had been trapped under twisted metal, shut in darkness even during the day, for hours before Julian had pulled her from the wreckage. Ever since then, she'd suffered an anxiety attack any time she was in the dark again.

She forced herself to take slow, deep breaths, and steadied her racing pulse. As she calmed down, she noticed the blackness was not complete. Flames, from candles burned low, flickered faintly—dispelling tiny circles of night.

She didn't need light to know that she was alone.

Julian was gone. She lifted a hand to her neck. Running her fingertips around her throat, she noted no puncture marks—no sticky blood clung to her skin. He'd kept his word; he hadn't hurt her. Yet. Could she trust him?

She lifted the blanket, and cool air rushed over her bare skin. *She was naked.* Despite the room's low temperature, heat suffused her body—with embarrassment and vestiges of the passion he'd drawn from her—from her soul. She'd never responded to any man the way she had to him.

But he wasn't a man—at least not *just* a man. He was so much more. More than she could handle.

Hands shaking, she jerked the sheet from the bed and wrapped it toga style around her. Her eyes adjusted to the darkness now, she searched the hardwood floor around the bed but could not find her dress. So she opened the doors of the antique wardrobe, but only a few men's shirts hung from the rod. She dropped the sheet in favor of one of the shirts, thrusting her arms into the long sleeves and doing up the buttons. The tails reached nearly to her knees, and she had to roll back the cuffs several folds in order to see her hands.

She continued her search through the drawers of an antique bureau, finding only a few boxer shorts and socks. From the sparse furnishings, she would guess this was not his primary residence. Where had he brought her?

Fumbling around in the faint candlelight, she found some thick drapes, but when she drew them back, she revealed only more aged brick wall. No window. No escape but for the door. Before she rattled the knob she knew it would not turn. A lock held it closed, trapping her inside. And him out?

Could she believe him? Was he only intent on protecting her? Or seducing her? Since he'd already done that, he didn't need to keep her. Unless his body, like hers, ached for more….

Her knees weak, she returned to the bed and sank to the edge of the mattress. He hadn't caused her reaction; it wasn't desire for him making her weak and vulnerable. It had to be hunger. He wasn't wrong—she hadn't been taking care of herself much lately.

Actually, she hadn't taken care of herself at all. If she had, she might not have fainted in his arms and wound up trapped in a dungeon—albeit an elegant, romantic one. The darkness spurred her panic again, but she fought it back, refusing to let fear control her. She couldn't let him—and her desire for him—control her, either.

She had to find a way out. Noticing the bedside table she had yet to search, she yanked open a drawer. Despite the candle burning atop the table, she didn't have enough light to see inside so she had to fumble through the contents. She pulled out a phone charger but could find no phone, only some papers she held near the candle to read. Take-out menus for restaurants in the downtown Zantrax area. The city in Michigan, which was even larger than Detroit, was hours from the suburban town where Sienna had lived with her grandparents.

How long had she been out that he'd had time to bring her here? Had he drugged her? Was that why she, who was always so cautious with men and especially with her heart, had made love with him so soon after meeting him?

Yet it wasn't soon. She'd known him a long time. And despite what he was, he was still her hero. Or he had been. She wasn't sure what he was now, nearly twenty years after pulling her from the wreckage. A photograph slipped from between the menus and fell picture-side up on the tabletop. Faces peered up at her from the yellowed snapshot. Familiar faces. Julian's handsome face and one that was eerily similar to hers, but the picture was aged. The embracing couples' vintage clothing and the antique car behind them, that was at least sixty years old, dated the photo.

Her grandmother and Julian had had a relationship? The thought churned in her empty stomach, and she pressed a hand over her mouth. Her palm held in the gasp that escaped when the door rattled open. She caught just a brief glimpse of the hall before he closed the door with his back, his hands busy with the tray he carried.

"You're awake," he said, his voice rough with a trace of disappointment. He'd pulled on just his pants, leaving his heavily muscled chest and arms bare.

"Yes…" She swallowed hard, fighting down the instant desire that he inspired in her. "I— I'm awake."

"And unharmed," he told her, his lips curving into that wicked grin again. "I told you I wouldn't hurt you."

She nodded, agreeing that he'd said the words, but she still wasn't convinced he would honor his claim. "Why did you bring me here?" she asked. "To seduce me?"

"I'm not sure who seduced whom," he teased her as he settled the tray onto the mattress. Fresh fruit overflowed a bowl; frothy whipped cream filled another. Champagne bubbled in flutes.

She gestured toward what he'd brought her. "I think it's pretty clear…" That he wanted to seduce her again. She crossed her legs, trying to fight the pressure that was already building inside her.

He shook his head. "No, it isn't…" He leaned forward and skimmed his fingers along her jaw. His voice low with awe, he murmured, "You are so beautiful…"

She lifted the photo she'd found and held it next to her face. "I look like my grandmother."

He didn't even glance at the picture, his mesmerizing gaze intent on her face. "You're even more beautiful."

Nana had always claimed the same thing; Sienna couldn't see it, as she studied the old photograph again. She only saw Julian's arm wrapped possessively around her grandmother's slender shoulders.

"Were you…" she choked on the word, but finally managed to utter it "…lovers?"

"No," he said, his voice firm with sincerity. "She was already engaged to your grandfather when we met. She would not betray him—no matter what I offered her."

"Immortality," she said, remembering the rambling story Nana had told on her deathbed. "I thought it was just the drugs talking…"

"If only it had been," he remarked, "if only I hadn't been so arrogant…"

He had every reason for arrogance. He was more handsome than any man she'd seen before—even on movie screens. "So you did…offer her immortality?" she asked.

"I never actually said the words…"

"But Nana knew," Sienna realized. "She just knew things. Grandpa said she had a gift." A gift Sienna wished she'd inherited so that she might be able to reveal Julian's true intentions.

"I wish my grandfather had believed that." He pushed a hand through his long hair, tangling the glossy strands. "But he didn't believe mortals have gifts."

"So he's a…?"

His mouth lifted, again, in that wicked grin. "You still can't say the word."

She still struggled to accept that she was awake, that she wasn't dreaming the whole thing…especially making love with him. The intensity of passion and pleasure…that had to have been a dream. But even now, the attraction simmered between them, causing her skin to tingle and her pulse to quicken. And he hadn't touched her again except with that dark gaze of his. "Everything seems so unreal," she admitted. Especially him and her attraction to him.

"I'm real," he assured her, as if he'd read her mind. "And to answer your question, yes, all Vossimers are."

Vampires.

Despite all the trouble his arrogance had caused, Julian had to know, "Is that why your grandmother turned me down?"

Sienna's blue eyes sparkled with amusement. "Her rejection stung?"

Regrettably that was all it had done. At least if he'd loved her, all the tragedy that had followed wouldn't have been so senseless.

· But Julian had never loved anyone. Maybe he wasn't capable—none of the Vossimers he knew had been. His parents had abandoned him to his grandfather when he was just a child. And Orson Vossimer hardly oozed affection. The man had always considered Julian a burden. Maybe Julian's problem was that *he* just wasn't lovable himself.

Sienna must have picked up on his thoughts for she leaned forward, her hand on his forearm. "Did you love her?"

He shook his head.

"That's what she chose over you," she explained. "Love."

"Over immortality?"

"She didn't regret her decision, not even at the last." Her face paled as if she was about to faint again as she added, "Not even when she was suffering so much…" Her skin cancer had metastasized, spreading to all her organs.

"I'm sorry," Julian said, covering her hand with his. "I'm sorry she had to suffer." His grandfather, who could not only telepathically communicate, could also sometimes predict the future. Julian suspected that was why Orson had let Carolina Briggs live as long as she had—because he'd "seen" her suffering. "That must have been horrible for her…and you."

She nodded as tears shimmered in her beautiful eyes.

"Here," he said, gesturing toward the tray, "I brought you something to eat."

The tears dried, and the amusement returned. "And champagne. Are you trying to get me drunk?"

He'd brought the champagne to celebrate…when she agreed to become his bride. But for once his arrogance deserted him. While her grandmother's rejection had only stung his pride, he worried that Sienna's might hurt more. He couldn't ask her yet—not until he was certain of her answer.

And her love.

While he wasn't convinced he could love, he was confident that…if he had time…he could make her think she loved him. Then, by the time she realized like everyone else had, that she didn't really love him, it would be too late.

If only Orson and the rest of the Underground would give him the time….

"I'm not trying to get you drunk," he assured her. "I'm trying to take care of you."

"And I told you I can take care of myself."

From the dark circles beneath her eyes and the thinness of her slight body, he doubted it. So he reached for the tray and held up a strawberry to her lips.

Instead of continuing to argue her self-sufficiency with him, she opened her mouth and sank her straight, white teeth into the ripe berry. Juice squirted out and trailed over her chin, down her throat.

His heart slammed against his ribs as his hunger overwhelmed him. He had never wanted to taste anyone with the urgency he wanted—*needed*—to taste her. He pulled the berry away and replaced the fruit with his lips, pressing them to the sweetness of hers. Her mouth opened again, her tongue sliding across his lip to touch his. The kiss wasn't enough to satisfy his hunger. He slid his mouth over her chin and down her throat.

Her fingers clenched in his hair, and she shivered. "Please…don't hurt me…"

"Never," he promised, even though he feared it was a vow he would eventually have to break. His fingers shook as he fought the buttons free on the shirt she wore—*his* shirt. Possessiveness gripped him, filling him with satisfaction. She was *his*. He parted the shirt then pushed it from her shoulders. His breath left his lungs in a ragged sigh. "You are so beautiful…"

Despite her thinness, she had generous curves. Full breasts, dark pink nipples tilting up from the honey-hued mounds. Soft hips sloped from a tiny waist. He skimmed his fingers down her sides, over her silky skin. She shivered again.

"You're cold," he said, cursing the fact he'd had to hide her here—underground. Even if he wasn't hiding her, he'd have to stay here…as the sun was bound to rise soon. Consignment to life in the dark, that was the curse of his existence. Could he ask her to share it?

She shook her head. "I'm not cold."

But he lifted the tray from the mattress, setting it atop the bedside table where she'd dropped her grandmother's picture. He hadn't kept it all these years to remember Carolina Briggs; he'd kept it to remember his own foolishness in asking anyone to become his bride.

When he reached for the blankets to pull them over her naked body, she caught his wrist, her nails nipping at his skin. "I'm not cold," she repeated, "I'm hungry."

Before he could retrieve the tray, she reached for the snap of his pants. A laugh rumbled first in his chest, then his throat. The vibration eased his urgency, calming his anxiety over their predicament. He hadn't laughed in so long.

Then she planted a palm against his chest and pushed him back on the mattress, and his laughter ceased, the tension and urgency returning to his body with painful intensity. But it wasn't fear driving him; it was passion.

"Who's the seducer now?" he asked, his words turning to a groan as she unzipped his fly and released his straining erection.

First she slid her fingertips down the length of him. Then she leaned over and ran her tongue over his engorged flesh. He tangled a hand in her hair, holding her to him as she closed her lips around the aching tip of his penis.

"Sienna!" Her passion surprised him. But her generosity should not have; she'd obviously grown used to putting others' needs over her own.

He couldn't take advantage of her. So he pushed her back, refusing to take the pleasure she offered with her mouth. And he made love to her body, kissing every inch of sweet skin. When his fangs scraped across a sensitive point, like the tip of her breast, or the dip of her navel, she moaned. If he bit her, he knew she'd enjoy it, but he didn't want to scare her. Her eyes, staring down at him, were wide with fear, but also excitement.

He kissed her like he had before, intimately, sliding his tongue into the heat of her desire. His own body ached and throbbed, demanding release. But he waited until she came, her hands clutching in his hair as she screamed his name. Then he pulled her to the edge of the high mattress. And he thrust inside her—again and again. She met him, rising off the bed, her legs wrapped around his waist, her hands in his hair then gripping his shoulders. She nipped the straining muscles in his neck as she came again, shuddering as her orgasm bubbled hot and sticky over him. Her inner muscles clutched his erection, squeezing and squeezing until he could control his need no longer.

Passion exploded with one last nearly violent thrust, and he came. "Sienna!"

They collapsed onto the bed, his face buried in the sweet temptation of her neck. He slid his mouth along her throat then parted his lips so his fangs scraped across her skin. "Sienna, let me turn you."

"What?" She tensed beneath him.

"Become a Vossimer," he urged her. "Become my wife."

Chapter 5

Sienna's heart clenched with excitement then dread as she remembered, "All Vossimers are vampires." She'd finally said the word, but she could never become one. "Why, Julian? Why do you want me to marry you?"

"It's the only way I can protect you."

She should have been relieved he hadn't professed love, because it was too soon and would have proved him a liar, yet disappointment squeezed her heart. She sucked in a shaky breath and asked, "Who are you protecting me from?"

His arms tightened around her, holding her closer as if he was using his body to shield her. "People who will hurt you."

"They'll do more than hurt me," she realized. "They intend to kill me. Why?"

"Because of what you know."

"About you?" She'd said it once, but she could not manage to utter the word again around the lump of emotion choking her. "About what you are?"

He nodded. "I'm not the only one."

"You told me that all Vossimers are," she recalled. "So you have family?"

A muscle twitched in his cheek. "Yes. Relatively speaking."

"You're not close then?"

"Not at all," he admitted. "But there are more than Vossimers. There's a whole Underground Society."

"I had no idea…" she murmured, stunned. "I would have never imagined…" Not only his existence, but his passion.

"You're not supposed to know. No mortal is."

She shivered as understanding dawned. "And that's why I'm in danger."

He sighed. "Any time a human has learned about our existence, bad things happen. The undead are destroyed."

The thought of him dead knocked the air from her lungs, filling her with a sense of loss even greater than she'd already known. "But…how…?"

"There are ways."

He might have wanted to spare her the image, but she closed her eyes and it was there—in her mind: Julian lying on the ground, a stake through his heart. She shuddered. "No…"

"When humans learn of our existence, they react

with fear. They think we pose a danger. So they try to eliminate that threat."

"You keep telling me that I'm in danger," she said, "that's why you brought me here." Why he'd proposed.

"Because you know. Because of what happened when other people found out, the Underground Society made a rule—for our protection."

"How many people have found out?" she asked, having to know how many mortals were killed—and how many Julian had personally killed.

Had she made love, not just with a vampire, but a cold-blooded killer? Goose bumps lifted her skin as dread chilled her to the bone.

"It was believed that your grandmother knew our secret," he said.

"But she died from a horrible disease," she said, flashing back to Nana's suffering. "No one killed her."

"No. There was actually no proof she knew…until the end."

"Until she told me."

He nodded then grimaced and admitted, "There was someone else who knew, who planned to write an exposé on the Secret Vampire Society. He was going to reveal our whereabouts and order our deaths."

Sienna's breath caught. "And this man? He was killed?"

Julian nodded. "Him and his wife."

"Was I alive when the murders took place?" she asked, wondering if she'd read about them. If the man had been a famous reporter or writer, his death could have been sensationalized, like her father's had been.

"You were seven," Julian answered, his deep voice raspy with emotion, "and in the backseat."

Her breath hissed out. "My father? How had he found out?"

"I don't believe your grandmother ever told him, but he inherited her gift. He knew things…he would have been better off never knowing. Then he investigated until he discovered other things—things you would have been better off that he never learned."

Grief pressed heavy on her heart. "I guess it's good that I didn't inherit that family gift—that I took after my grandfather instead."

"He was a simple man," Julian said.

"A good man," Sienna defended him as she twisted on her finger the engagement ring that her grandfather had put on her grandmother's.

"You're wearing that ring," Julian observed.

She nodded. "Nana gave it to me, wanted the man I marry to put it on my left hand."

"Marry me," he urged her again.

She shook her head, tears burning her eyes. "I can't…"

"Because you can't forgive my part in the accident?"

"What was your part?" she had to know, her stomach churning with revulsion. Had she made love with—not once but twice—the man responsible for her parents' deaths?

"I didn't stop it." He dragged in a ragged breath. "I tried…but I was too late. Too late to save them. And too much of a coward to save you."

"But you did," she reminded him. "You saved my

life." She wished he could have saved her parents, too, but she believed he'd tried.

"I got lucky—that you weren't more seriously hurt," he said, "because I couldn't get to you right away."

"I know—the crash was horrible. The car was so far down in the ravine that it was a wonder you found me at all."

"I saw the car go over," he admitted. "But the sun was coming up. I couldn't get to you…not without risking my own life."

Sienna tensed, shocked.

"So much for being your hero, huh?" he said, and he lifted his arm and let her slide away from him. "I'm sorry. But I can't be out in the sun…and live…"

"So much for being undead," she murmured.

"Is that why you won't marry me?" he asked. "Because of what I am?"

She wasn't certain if he was referring to his being a vampire or his not being the hero she'd believed him to be for the past twenty years. "No. I made my grandmother a promise on her deathbed."

"To wear this ring?" He ran a fingertip over the diamond then over the scar on his chin.

"She did that? My grandmother?"

His lips curved into that wickedly sexy grin. "She didn't like what I said about your grandfather."

"She was feisty." Sienna wished she possessed her grandmother's spirit, as well as her face.

"She was stubborn," Julian said. "You can't be stubborn. The rest of the Underground will find us. I won't be able to save you this time."

"Unless I become your bride…" She glanced down at the diamond. Could she let this man—this one whose interest in her grandmother had caused her family so much pain—switch the ring to her left hand? She shook her head. "I can't…"

"You're exhausted," Julian said, brushing his fingertip under her eyes, over the dark circles she hadn't been able to hide with makeup. "Sleep on it."

She nodded and lowered her lids. But no matter how much rest she got, she wouldn't change her mind. She had made her grandmother a promise. Like Carolina Briggs, Sienna would only marry for love. She couldn't marry a man who offered just protection or even immortality. She could only marry the man who offered her his heart.

She couldn't marry Julian Vossimer…even if that decision killed her.

She was gone. Julian didn't need to open his eyes to confirm Sienna's absence. After what he'd revealed, he wasn't surprised that she would have slipped away while he slept. He should have locked the door behind himself, but he'd been juggling the tray of food that sat beside the bed, mostly untouched. The champagne still filled the glasses, but no bubbles rushed to the rim. It had gone flat.

"Sienna?" he called out. Maybe she could hear him the way that Orson could. Maybe she had her grandmother's gift, but had been unaware until now, as she'd been unaware of the kind of man he really was.

She must hate him—so much that even if she had the gift, she'd block him from her mind. And from her heart.

"Sienna!" His voice cracked with urgency. He had

to find her. Yet even though the bedroom was dark, all the candles burned out, he knew it was day. Because he had to fight for the energy to leave the bed.

Even if she wouldn't accept his proposal, he had to find a way to save her. He couldn't let the others kill her…because that would kill him as surely as his leaving the darkness.

Moments later, he climbed the stairs to street level. Light penetrated low-hanging gray clouds and the shower of falling snow. He lifted the collar of his trench coat and slid dark glasses onto his nose. But those precautions were ineffectual as the daylight seeped through his clothes, through his skin and weakened his spirit— draining his soul.

"Sienna…"

His eyes already squinted against the light. He closed them fully and blanked his mind…until she appeared. First as she'd been in his bed—naked and passionate. And then he found her—in the present. In her house, sobbing softly….

She didn't cry for him; he was sure of it, convinced that she hated him now that she knew everything about him. As Orson had said, he was too much trouble. He'd brought Sienna nothing but pain.

And now pain filled him, burning him alive—zapping his strength. But he couldn't turn back. Because he could see more than Sienna; he could see what she had yet to realize—that she was not alone.

Chapter 6

Tears streaked down Sienna's face while sobs burned her throat. She'd already broken her promise to her grandmother. She wasn't supposed to cry. But these tears weren't just over missing Nana; she missed *him*.

"That's another promise I broke," she admitted miserably as she twisted the ring on the finger of her right hand. "I love a man who doesn't love me."

While she hadn't been able to keep all the promises she'd made Nana, she would keep at least one of them. She glanced toward the tree, which stood before the bay window in the front parlor. Its finely needled branches were bare of lights and ornaments. Sienna had barely found the time to buy the tree; she hadn't been able to decorate it before Nana had passed.

But she'd promised that she would, that she'd deck the halls and celebrate the holiday. She wouldn't let another loss, however devastating, destroy her. She was stronger than that—stronger even than the threat of which Julian had warned. Dashing her tears away with the backs of her hands, Sienna dragged her weary body from the chair. The last thing she felt like doing, after taking the train from Zantrax, was decorating. But this, at least, was one promise she could keep.

Clad in the red velvet dress she'd found in the bathroom of Julian's apartment, Sienna hesitated at the door to the cellar stairs. Jeans and a sweatshirt would be more appropriate attire for digging through cobwebs and dusty boxes. But Nana had loved the velvet dress. And from the desire in his eyes as he'd stripped it from her, so had Julian.

Every thought returned to Julian, like Sienna ached to return to him. Maybe she could get back before dark, before he awakened and noticed that she'd gone. But could she, who feared the dark, turn into a creature who dwelt only in darkness? Even now, panic pressed on her chest as she opened the door to basement. Shadows fell across the steep steps that led to the rough concrete floor.

She'd always hated the cellar, but something more than panic assailed her. A sense of foreboding joined her usual fear, and her legs shook as she descended the rickety stairwell. "Hello?" she called out, as goose bumps lifted on the skin on her arms and the nape of her neck. Instinctively, she knew she was not alone. "Hello?"

Had Julian braved the daylight to come to her? No, she would have known the minute he was near; her body would have reacted, with heat and anticipation, to the closeness of his. But she was not alone. "Who's there?"

"Maybe you do have your grandmother's gift," someone mused from the shadows. The voice was feminine and familiar.

"Ingrid?" The hospice nurse had helped out with Nana at night, so that Sienna had been able to get some rest. She had helped only at night, coming by just after the sun had gone down. Was she one of them? Of the Secret Vampire Society? "What are you doing here?"

"I think you know," the beautiful woman said, her dark eyes glowing eerily in the shadows.

Fear pounded in Sienna's veins. Julian had told her the truth; she was in danger. Maybe she could convince the vampiress that she had no knowledge of their society. "No. I expected to see you at the funeral home—not here."

"I was there," Ingrid said. "At the funeral home *and* when your grandmother told you about us."

Sienna shook her head and infused confusion in her voice as she asked, "About us? I don't understand."

Ingrid's lips, either naturally or painted a deep red, curved into a slight smile. "About Julian Vossimer. She told you about Julian."

"She never said his name," Sienna maintained. "Not that I paid much attention to anything she was saying at the end. She wasn't making any sense." A twinge of pain struck her heart as she remembered, "She was out of her mind with pain."

"She was completely lucid, right until the end,"

Ingrid said, with a trace of respect for Carolina Briggs. "She got you to make some big promises."

"To celebrate Christmas."

"That's how I knew you'd come down here," the nurse explained.

"To get the decorations." She suspected Ingrid had actually come down to the cellar in order to get away from the sunshine streaming in through the upstairs windows. "The tree looks so naked…"

The image flitting through her mind wasn't of tree branches, though. She imagined Julian instead, how he'd looked—sculpted muscles rippling beneath taut skin, as he had moved over her—then inside her. Despite the dampness of the basement, heat suffused Sienna, spreading throughout her body. She had never been satisfied—*pleasured*—as thoroughly by any other man, and she wanted him again.

Would she even get to see him one last time—now that she'd been found?

"You look like her, you know," Ingrid remarked from where she lurked yet in the shadows.

"My grandmother?"

"This angel." The vampiress held up an ethereal blond doll. "I can understand why he fell for you."

Sienna's heart kicked against her ribs. "Who?"

The slight smile flashed again, but still those dark eyes glowed eerily—with madness and an anguish that struck a chord within Sienna. "You're beautiful," Ingrid said, "not stupid. You know Julian has fallen for you."

"If I believed that, I wouldn't be here," Sienna pointed out. "I'd still be with him." In his bed, in his arms—her head against his chest, his heart beating steadily beneath her cheek. Why had she left him? Then she remembered. "He doesn't love me."

"I can understand your doubts," Ingrid admitted and continued as if they were friends commiserating about men. "Julian wouldn't have professed his love. He probably doesn't even realize he loves you yet. Men can be so dense." Now the anguish thickened her voice. "They sometimes deny their feelings until it's too late…."

"Was it too late for you?" Sienna asked.

Ingrid released a shuddery breath. "I heard the words. Despite the stake buried in his heart, he managed to tell me he loved me. It was the last thing he ever said."

"I'm sorry…."

"You should be," Ingrid said, rage chasing the sadness from her voice and eyes. "Your father is the one who drove in the stake."

Sienna gasped as another one of her idols fell. "My dad? You're talking about his exposé? I thought he died *before* it was published."

"Julian told you about the exposé?"

She nodded.

"But he didn't tell you what your father did," Ingrid said. "He wanted to spare you the truth."

"What is the truth?" Sienna had to know.

"My…Michael…was your father's source for the article. Michael was so trusting. He didn't understand that he was putting us all in danger—until it was too late, until your father murdered him. He didn't just write the article. He killed Michael. My lover's blood was on your father's hands."

"You got your revenge," Sienna said, suspecting her father's blood was on Ingrid's hands. That the vampiress was the one who was responsible for Sienna's parents' deaths. "You don't need to hurt me."

"You're human. You can't be trusted," Ingrid insisted.

"You were around me for months," Sienna reminded her. "You know me…you know I would never hurt anyone."

"You've already hurt Julian," Ingrid said.

Sienna shook her head. "No…" He was the last person she wanted to hurt.

"You rejected him."

"H-how do you know?"

"Because you're here, and he isn't," Ingrid pointed out.

"That's because he doesn't love me…" That was why she'd turned him down, she realized. Not because she wasn't certain she could become what he was… but because she couldn't even consider changing without his love.

Ingrid shook her head, as if disgusted. "The guy gave up his life for you. What more does he have to give up to prove his love?"

Shock and pain staggered Sienna so that she had to grip the stair railing or tumble down the last few steps to the concrete floor. "No! He's not dead."

"Not yet. But Orson Vossimer warned him. If he didn't kill you, he would be killed."

"Orson Vossimer? He's related to Julian. How could he kill him?"

"Orson Vossimer is Julian's grandfather. And he gave Julian another option besides death. He could turn you."

And Sienna had refused. "I didn't know…"

"It's too late now," Ingrid said. "You're both going to die."

And Sienna would never have the chance to tell Julian that she loved him.

Light blind, Julian staggered through the house. Every muscle ached in protest of his movements, but he forced himself to continue, feeling his way along the walls. "Sienna!"

"Julian?"

Her voice, quavering with fear and shock, drew him toward an open door. He stumbled, nearly falling down the stairs.

"Julian!" An arm slid around his waist, a warm body wedging against his side to support his weight. "Oh, my God…what happened to you?"

"You," Ingrid said with blatant disgust. "You happened to him." Then the vampiress turned toward him. "Saving Orson the trouble of killing you?"

The only one he wanted to save was Sienna, but he could barely stand or talk. He didn't have to be a nurse, like Ingrid, to know that he was dying. But with his last ounce of strength, he would fight to protect the woman he loved. "Leave…her…be…" he murmured.

"You're in no condition to be issuing orders," Ingrid said with a vicious laugh.

"Julian, you have to leave," Sienna whispered urgently. "Just leave…" Her small hands pushed at his chest, trying to shove him up the stairs.

He swayed and stumbled back a step. But other

hands were there, not to catch him, but to hold him. He didn't need to turn around to know that Ingrid had summoned her reinforcements. He lowered his head, focusing on Sienna. She stared up at him, her blue eyes wide with fear and glistening with unshed tears. "I'm sorry," he said.

She shook her head. "You have no reason to be sorry. It's my fault. I should have listened to you."

"I didn't tell you what you needed to hear," he said. But he couldn't say it now—he couldn't say in front of all these people the words he should have given her when they were alone and in each other's arms. He knew now what it would have taken for her to accept his proposal. His love.

"I'm sorry I'm not your hero…."

Chapter 7

Sienna's heart pounded a frantic rhythm. And she couldn't stop trembling—not just with fear, but from the cold. After night had fallen, they'd left the cellar, and they'd flown...to wherever they were now. But they hadn't used a plane, or a helicopter or any other type of machine. They'd just...flown. They hadn't flapped their arms or kicked their legs, but somehow they'd moved through the frigid night air.

Sienna was surprised they hadn't killed her then. The man who'd carried her would have had only to drop her. The fall would have killed her, leaving her body broken beyond recognition.

But Ingrid had ordered them delivered here—to another underground dwelling even more opulent than the apartment to which Julian had brought her. He lay now, unconscious, on a hard marble floor. Sienna knelt at his side, stroking her fingers over the chiseled angle of his cheekbone and jaw. "Wake up. Please wake up…"

He wasn't just sleeping. She wasn't even sure he was breathing anymore. So she moved her hand to his throat and felt for a pulse. But her fingers were numb and his skin so cold, she could find no reassuring beat.

"Julian," she whispered.

The men who'd flown them here stood around, glaring at her as she'd already been warned to keep quiet. They were beyond big, beyond her ability to fight. If only Julian were awake…

"He's dying," Ingrid said, her heels clicking against the marble as she walked back into the room from wherever she'd been.

And it's all my fault. Guilt clutched at Sienna. If she'd listened to him, if she'd believed him—they'd both be safe now.

"It is all your fault, girl," a man's deep voice spoke to her thoughts.

Tearing her gaze from Julian's pale face, she glanced up and then gasped. "You…" He looked so much like his "grandson"—even approximately the same age.

"We don't age, girl," he explained. "But we can die." He knelt near Julian and brushed a trembling hand through his grandson's hair. "That's why it's too risky for humans to learn of our existence. It makes us vulnerable."

"I won't hurt anyone," Sienna promised.

"Too late," the man snapped, as he rose to his feet and stared down at her. "You've already hurt my family."

"Your honor."

"Twice now," he said. "Vossimers are Underground royalty. Royalty does not offer marriage to commoners only to have those commoners reject them."

If Vossimers were Underground royalty, Julian was their prince and this man considered himself king. Regrettably, so did the burly men who hung on his every word as if he were issuing royal decrees.

"I'm sorry," she murmured demurely. "I was wrong to turn Julian down. Help him, please…"

"It's too late for my grandson," Orson said, whatever affection he'd betrayed when he'd petted Julian's hair was gone now. "He has brought dishonor to our family too many times. And he's brought danger to the rest of the Underground."

"It wasn't his fault," Sienna defended him. "He never said anything to my grandmother. She had a gift. She knew things. Ask Ingrid."

The older Vossimer turned toward the beautiful vampiress. "Is this true?"

After a slight hesitation, she nodded. "But it doesn't change what happened. *She* knows our secret. *She* cannot live."

Pride lifted Sienna to her feet. "I don't care what you do to me. Just save him. Save Julian."

Orson Vossimer narrowed his eyes and studied her. "You act as though you care about my grandson."

"I love him," she admitted.

The older man laughed. "You think me a fool. That I will believe your lies?"

"I love him," Sienna insisted. "I'm not lying."

"Then you're the fool, girl," Vossimer said.

"He's a good man," she defended her lover again. "He's my hero." No matter what he believed; she knew the truth now.

"Then why would you turn him down when he offered you marriage, when he offered you a way to keep your life…for eternity?"

She sucked in a shaky breath. "Fear." Not just of the dark, but of the risk of giving her heart to a man who wouldn't give his in return.

"You are a fool, girl."

"Yes," she agreed. "I should have said yes. If I could go back…" She glanced down at Julian's lifeless body and remembered the passion with which he'd made love to her. "Please, help him…"

"It's too late, girl," Orson said, emotion turning his voice into a rough rasp. "It's too late…"

"Ingrid," she turned to the other woman. "You're a nurse. You must know what to do…how to save him…"

"His life is ebbing away," Ingrid said with a weary sigh of her own.

"But he's not dead yet." She refused to believe that, refused to let him go. "Please, help him," she beseeched the other woman. "*You* can help him."

Ingrid shook her head. "No, I can't. But you might be able to…"

"How?"

"Let him take your life."

"He can have it," Sienna offered. If not for him, she wouldn't have lived as long as she had. No one would have ever found the wreckage of her family's car. She wouldn't have survived without him. "I owe him…my life."

"Is this a trick, girl?" Orson asked.

"This is love." Love was selfless, like Julian endangering himself to find her and try to rescue her. It was her turn to rescue him—even if it killed her.

They're going to kill her. The horrific thought chased the blackness of unconsciousness from Julian's mind. He fought the heaviness of his lids to blink open his eyes, gritty with fatigue.

"Sienna!" He tried to shout her name, but it escaped as a weak rasp. "Sienna!"

A soft hand brushed hair back from his face. "I'm here," she assured him, with a sigh of relief. "And so are you…"

She blurred before his weary eyes, and he blinked again until he could clearly see her. Even tense and pale with concern and fear, her face was beautiful. Then his gaze moved beyond her to register their surroundings— the marble floors and walls. "We're at my grandfather's."

She nodded. "He had us brought here…to this bedroom…"

"My bedroom," Julian said, with a surge of hope. "Are we alone?"

A laugh, high-pitched with a hint of hysteria, slipped from her lips. "You can't want to…"

"I will always want you," he said.

"But you're so sick."

If that was all he was, he could rally the strength to help her. But his situation was worse than that. Her situation didn't have to be the same. "I can tell you how to get out of here," he said.

She shook her head. "I'm not leaving you!"

"There's a bathroom behind that door…" He tried to lift his arm to gesture, but his limb was too heavy, his muscles too weak to move. His lungs ached as he struggled for breath with ragged pants. "There's a vent in the ceiling. If you climb on the vanity, you'll be able to reach it."

She pressed her fingers across his lips. "Shh…save your strength."

What strength? If he had any left, he could carry her into the bathroom, lift her to the vent and help her get away from the Underground. But once again, he was too weak to be her true hero.

"I'm *not* leaving you," she said, her voice firm and her statement implacable.

He managed to curl his fingers into the curve of her hip. "You *have* to…" He pushed her. "You have to go. Now."

"There's no time," she said.

"There's time," he argued, "for you to get away." But how long could she stay hidden from Ingrid and Orson?

"I'm not leaving without you."

"I can't move," he admitted with frustration and stinging pride.

"You don't have to do anything," she said as she wrapped her arms around his neck. "But bite me…"

He tensed; maybe he was so weak that he'd imagined what she'd said. "What?"

"*Turn* me, Julian."

He moved his head, to shake it, but she'd put her

neck there so that his lips brushed across the silky skin of her throat. "No…it's too great a risk."

"They're going to kill us both if you don't," she reminded him.

"But I might kill you," he said, dread twisting his stomach in knots. "I've never turned anyone before." And fatigue had stolen his usual cocky assurance, so that he wasn't convinced, even if he wasn't so weak, that he'd know how to turn her without killing her.

"You're going to die if you don't," she said. "Ingrid told me that this is your only chance—to use my life to save yours."

He shook his head. "I can't…"

"Julian, you're dying now. This is your one chance. I'm your one chance."

"No…"

"I love you, Julian."

Her words suffused him with heat and passion. "You love me?"

She nodded. "Yes."

"But you left me." Pain, more emotional than physical, staggered him as he remembered waking alone and finding her gone. "I thought you couldn't accept my part in your parents' tragic deaths. I thought you hated me…"

"I had to get away to think," she explained, "to consider the life you offered me."

"The life you rejected when you rejected me."

"I rejected the life—not you," she insisted. "We made love…twice…" She entwined her fingers in his hair. "I love you."

He wanted to believe her, but nobody had ever said

those words to him let alone meant them. Did she? Or was she only trying to help him because she was used to taking care of people?

"I only take care of people I care about," she said.

"What?" Shocked, he met her gaze, her blue eyes wide with awe.

"I can hear your thoughts," she told him, as shocked as he was.

"You have your grandmother's gift."

She nodded. "I just realized that now. I wish I would have realized it sooner. If I could have heard your thoughts earlier, maybe I wouldn't have left you and then you wouldn't have had to risk your life in the daylight. It's my fault, Julian, that you're dying. You have to use me to save you."

"Sienna…"

"If you don't, we're both going to die anyway," she said, "because I'm not leaving you."

"C'mon, Sienna, you can go out the vent," he urged her. "You can save yourself."

"For the moment. You think they won't track me down again? Where am I supposed to go? I have no place else to go—no one I want to be with but you." She kissed him, her lips pressing against his until he opened his mouth. Then she dipped her tongue between his lips, sliding it across the sharp tips of his fangs.

Hunger stirred within Julian, but it was nothing in comparison to the power of his love for her. "Sienna, if this doesn't work—"

"If it does, we can be together forever," she pointed out. "Unless that isn't what you want…?"

His heart contracted at the image she painted—the image of the two of them, in each other's arms, for eternity. Making love, making each other laugh—making each other happy. "It's what I want—more than anything else in this world, more than my own life. I can't…"

"You have to," she begged him. "Before it's too late for us. You have to—" And she kissed him again, first his lips. Then she slid her mouth over his chin and along the line of his clenched jaw.

He wanted her so badly. Not just now, but forever. "Are you sure, Sienna?" he asked.

"Absolutely," she assured him. Her fingers in his hair, she tugged up his head until his lips brushed across her throat. A moan slipped from between her lips. "Please…turn me…"

His heart, which had been beating weakly, kicked against his ribs—with anticipation and fear. "This might hurt."

"Just do it," she urged. "Just…bite me…"

He rubbed his lips back and forth across her throat, lifting goose bumps on her skin. She shivered. "Julian…"

He curled back his lips and pressed his fangs against her skin. And pressed harder until her skin broke.

She gasped, her breath hissing out between her teeth. But when he moved to pull back, she tightened her fingers in his hair and clutched him to her. "Turn me…"

He couldn't argue, not with her sweet taste sliding over his tongue. Heat and passion and love filled him as he drank. Too much or too little? The line was fine. One way would kill her; the other would leave her human and in danger of the Underground Society killing her.

Reenergized with her spirit, he pulled away from her. Her body had gone limp against him. He rolled her onto her back on the mattress and leaned over her. Her eyes had closed, her thick lashes lying against her pale skin. His hand shaking, he stroked his fingers over her cheek. "Sienna!"

Her skin had paled to a porcelain so clear her veins shone beneath the thin surface. Her pulse barely moved in her throat. Had he killed her?

"Sienna!"

The bedroom door squeaked open on rusty hinges. "Julian," his grandfather called his name. "You're all right?"

He shook his head, his eyes burning as he studied Sienna's beautiful face. "No, I'm not all right."

Strong fingers squeezed his shoulder. "You're alive. She's not—that's what needed to happen."

"She's not dead!" Not yet. Although faintly, her heart beat beneath the palm he pressed to her chest. "She can't die! She can't…"

She'd promised him eternity.

"If it's meant to be—if you're meant to be—she'll come back to you," Orson assured him.

"We're meant to be," Julian insisted as he stroked her hair back from her face. "We're meant to be."

"You have to prepare yourself," his grandfather warned him. "In case she doesn't make it."

Finally Julian tore his gaze from her and focused on the man who'd raised him in the ways of the Underground. "If she doesn't make it, neither will I."

"You say that now, but you'll get over her…like you got over her grandmother."

"I won't. I love Sienna." And yet he'd never given her the words. He'd never proved his love—like she had proved hers. For him she'd given up her life.

Chapter 8

Light flickered, glowing through Sienna's closed lids—calling her back from the darkness. Her body ached in protest as she shifted under the blankets pulled to her chin, her muscles weak and cramped. But the pain was good; the pain convinced her she wasn't dead.

Unless this was hell.

She dragged her eyes open to a room bathed in candlelight, as it had been the first time he'd brought her here. Plaster walls rose to that ornate coffered ceiling with the chandelier hanging low and dark above the bed. This wasn't hell; this was where she'd found heaven in Julian's arms.

Julian! Had it worked—had he'd drunk enough of her spirit to revive his dying body? "Julian!"

"Shh…" a deep voice murmured, then strong arms closed around her, pulling her tight against a muscular chest. "I'm here."

"You're alive!"

"And so are you…" His breath escaped in a shuddery sigh of relief. Lips skimmed across her cheek then brushed over her mouth. "You're alive!"

She blinked again, unable to believe that they were together. Free. "He let us go?" she asked, confusion muddling her weary mind.

"Yes."

Because Julian had done what his grandfather had wanted. He'd taken the only option the old man had given him besides her death. She glanced down at herself, her arms bare as she pulled them from beneath the blankets. Her throat dry, she swallowed hard and managed only, "Am I…?"

"You're back to not being able to say it?" he teased, his lips curving into that wicked grin.

"I could accept your being one," she said. "But me…" How could she have become what she didn't understand?

"You didn't think it through," he said, worry furrowing his brow.

"I thought only of you, of saving you," she admitted. "I didn't care about myself."

"That's why I love you," he said, "so much."

"I know you love me," she assured him. "Going out in the sunlight, you risked your life for me. You proved it."

"That last time I had," he agreed, but guilt haunted his dark eyes, "but I could have saved you from the wreck earlier and I waited…"

She reached up, pressing her fingers across his lips. "Shh…if you'd come out in daylight then, you would have died. And I would have died, too. To get me out, you had to pull apart that twisted metal—no human could have managed that. You wouldn't have had the strength to do that if you'd come out during the day." She narrowed her eyes, as she noticed her fingers—her ringless fingers on her right hand.

Julian lifted her left hand from the comforter. "The ring is here. I moved it."

"To my left hand?" She stared at the ring, which glinted in the faint candlelight. "But I turned you down."

"Because you didn't think I loved you," he guessed. Correctly.

"How do you know me so well?" she asked.

"We have a connection."

"Because you have my blood?"

"We had a connection even before that," he insisted. "We've had a connection for years. That was why I asked you to marry me—because I couldn't lose that connection. I couldn't lose you."

He had loved her—even before he'd realized it, as Ingrid had suggested.

"So why didn't you ask me again? At your grandfather's house?"

"I didn't know if I'd make it. I didn't know if either of us would make it. And I didn't know what I had to offer you," he explained. "And every minute you've been unconscious, I regretted not asking, not moving this ring to your left hand when you were awake and could answer me."

"So ask me again," she suggested although, from how she ached with exhaustion, she still wasn't convinced that she could survive the turning. Or hadn't she been turned at all? But before she could open her mouth to take back her advice, Julian slid off the bed and dropped to his knees beside it.

His hand grasping her left one, where the diamond twinkled, he asked, "Will you become my bride, Sienna Briggs?"

She focused first on the ring, then on his face, where the diamond-shaped scar marred the masculine perfection of his cleft chin. "Are you sure?"

"Sienna!" he exclaimed, his face paling with shock. "I'm so sure. I love you so much."

The words warmed her heart and curved her lips into a smile. But…

"That wasn't what I was referring to—I mean, the ring? Are you sure this is the ring you want me to wear…as *your* fiancée, as *your* bride?"

He stared down at the ring, too, now. "Oh, my God, I didn't think… Did you want me to buy you a new ring? One that I picked out?"

She shook her head, tears stinging her eyes, as she remembered her grandmother, using the last bit of her fading strength, to slide the ring onto her finger. "No." If she had believed she would be strong enough to risk her heart again, she would have wanted to wear this ring. "This is the one I want. It symbolizes the greatest love I'd ever known…"

"Until now," he said, "until ours."

Her heart warmed more as it filled with the love of

which he spoke. Their love. The greatest love she would ever know.

"But this ring doesn't mean the same thing to you that it does to me," she said. She managed to raise her hand to touch her fingertip to the scar on his chin. "To you it means rejection. To your grandfather it means dishonor."

"Your grandmother and I—we weren't meant to be," he said. "I think I even knew that then. I was just being an arrogant jerk. She had every right to hit me."

"Yes, she did. You insulted my grandfather—the man she loved more than life itself."

"More than the eternal life I offered her."

"It wasn't enough. You didn't love her."

"I didn't know that I could love," he said. "I didn't think I was capable until I met you. This ring—" he slid his thumb over the sharp points of it "—means something to me, too. It reminds me how much I changed— how much *you* changed me. It represents our love, too."

Tears blurred the ring, and his handsome face, from Sienna's gaze. "Yes, it does." And her grandmother's gift had been accurate again—that the right man would come along someday and slide it onto Sienna's real ring finger.

"That's the right answer," Julian said, "but to the wrong question."

She blinked back the tears. "What?"

"You haven't answered my first question," he reminded her. "Please, woman, put me out of my misery and respond to my proposal. Will you marry me?"

"Yes!" She tried to lift up from the pillow, but her body was limp, her muscles weak. "If only I were stronger, I would marry you now. Right this minute."

Because she wanted to be part of him…for the eternity he'd promised her. Fear tempered her happiness; she doubted that the "turning" had worked. Instead of eternal life, she would have to leave him…like her grandparents and parents had left her—to death.

"I'm sorry," she murmured. She'd taught him how to love, only to leave him—only to leave him to the anguish she'd had to endure when she'd lost the ones she'd loved. "I'm sorry…"

Panic pressed on Julian's lungs, so that he struggled for breath. Like Sienna struggled for breath. He could not lose her now. "You have no reason to be sorry," he assured her. He was the one who'd messed up—as usual.

"I'd hoped it would work…that we could be together…forever," she said. "But I'm so tired…" Her thick lashes brushed against the dark circles beneath her eyes as her lids closed.

He couldn't let her slip into unconsciousness again. He couldn't lose her again. He cupped her cheek in his palm. "Come on, Sienna, stay with me."

She blinked her eyes open, giving him hope. She hadn't slipped away yet.

And he wouldn't let her. He would do anything to keep her with him. "I know how you can get stronger," he said. "Use me." Like she had insisted he use her.

"What do you mean?" she asked, her blue eyes still dim with fatigue.

She wasn't dead yet. But he'd hurt her. His stomach clenched with dread and regret.

"I want you to do the same thing to me," he explained, with sensitivity to her unease about the vampire lifestyle, "that you had me do to you."

She shook her head. "I don't think I can. I'm going to have to find another way…to live…"

"There are other ways," he assured her. "We don't *feast* off people for sustenance. But I'm not talking about sustenance. I'm talking about survival—and about the connection between your soul and mine. It can only be complete when the same blood flows through us."

"It does."

"No, I have yours," he clarified, "but you don't have mine. Take *mine*."

"Julian…" She sighed. "I don't even know how. I don't have—"

He kissed her, deeply, sliding his tongue through her parted lips, stroking it over hers before tracing the line of her teeth. Her tongue followed the path of his then she tensed. So he pulled back.

"I have them," she murmured, in shock. "I have fangs…"

"It worked." He hadn't been entirely convinced himself until now. He had actually turned her. But she was still so pale—so weak. He could still lose her…if she didn't do as he asked.

"You're as surprised as I am."

He tensed, startled that she'd read him so easily. "What?"

Her lips curved into that faint smile. "I can hear you—your thoughts. Remember?"

Their connection was complete already. But it had

to last. "Then you should remember what happened the last time you didn't do as I asked."

A grimace momentarily twisted her delicate features. "I almost got us both killed."

"So obey me, woman."

"Obey?" she asked as she lifted a blond brow. "That won't be part of our vows."

"We won't be able to exchange those vows if you don't get stronger," he reminded her. "Use me to regain your strength."

"Julian…"

He did as she had, just the day before, he leaned forward and pressed his neck against her lips. "Bite me…"

Her lips parted, the heat of her faint breath warm against his skin. His body tensed again, with desire, with desperate need of hers. He wanted her completely—body and soul and her indomitable spirit. "Come on, Sienna."

"I can't…"

"You have to…for us," he urged her then groaned as her teeth nipped his skin.

She stopped and moved her mouth away. "I hurt you."

"No," he assured as he joined her on the bed, pressing his lower body into her hips so that she could feel his arousal. "You only hurt me by stopping. Don't stop this time."

She lifted her arms, wrapping them around his shoulders, and pulled him fully down on her. Then she sank her new fangs through his skin, into his throat, and she drank him in the way he'd drunk her.

Instead of feeling drained by her possession, Julian

felt energized—completely invigorated. He vibrated with passion for her. "Sienna…"

She pulled her teeth from his skin and licked the small wound she'd created. "I feel…"

"What?" he asked, rolling them both to their sides so he could see her face. Her skin, once so pale, was now flushed, and her blue eyes sparkled.

"I feel alive."

And for the first time since he'd tried to turn her, she looked alive. Vibrantly alive.

"You're beautiful," he said, his hand shaking as he palmed her cheek. "So beautiful…"

"You're beautiful," she said, her steady fingers clawing at the buttons of his shirt to open it. "You're perfect. And you're mine."

"All yours," he assured her with a chuckle as she shoved his shirt from her shoulders. He reached between them and dragged the blankets off her, baring her to his sight…and touch. He'd taken off her dress, so that she wore only those tantalizing scraps of lace. For the moment.

He intended to take them off her soon. But first he rose from the bed. Or tried to. Sienna clutched his shoulders, then his waist and murmured in protest.

"You're not going anywhere," she told him.

He shook his head as he unclasped his belt and dropped his jeans and boxers. "I'm not going anywhere—not without you. We're spending eternity together, my love."

"I wonder if that'll be long enough," she teased with a mischievous twinkle in her eye.

"Long enough?"

"To do everything I want to do to you." She reached for him, her hands sliding over the muscles of chest then his hips to his straining erection. First she stroked her fingers down his length, then she closed her lips around him and sucked him deep in her mouth. Her fangs scraped over the sensitive flesh.

He groaned, as passion like he'd never known surged through him. "Sienna!" He tried to pull away so he could reach for her.

But she was strong now, stronger than she'd been. And she grasped his butt, holding him to her—as she tortured him with her lips and tongue and the tips of her new fangs. He tangled his fingers in her hair and pulled, but it was too late. As her lips slipped down the length of him, he came, his legs shaking, his body shuddering as his orgasm spilled into the warmth of her mouth.

She licked her lips and lay back on the bed, as if she were satisfied. But he shook his head. She'd no idea the satisfaction he intended to give her.

"Promises, promises," she teased, speaking to his thoughts.

He joined her on the bed, pushing her into the mattress with his body—tense again already with desire for his fiancée. And he kissed her, tasting his own desire on her lips and tongue. Their teeth clinked, scraping across each other's—raising the hair on the nape of his neck. "Just when I thought I couldn't love you more…"

"You love me more," she said, scraping her nails down the rippling muscles of his back.

He dipped his head, nuzzled her neck.

"Bite me," she invited him.

He shook his head. "I want to taste you another way." He skimmed his lips down her throat to the slopes of her breasts. With just the tip of his tongue, he teased each pebbled point. Then he suckled the nipple deep into his mouth, his fangs nipping lightly into the soft flesh of her breast.

She moaned and shifted beneath him, pressing her hips into his—rubbing her damp curls against the erection that strained again to possess her.

But he denied himself the pleasure of burying himself inside her. Instead he moved again, sliding down her body until he could taste her desire for him. He pushed his tongue through her folds, dipping inside the moist heat. She arched again and clutched her fingers at his head, clasping his mouth to her so tightly that his fangs pressed against her mound.

She moaned and shifted and came, pouring honey into his mouth. Burning with desire for her, he rose up and thrust himself inside her.

She arched so abruptly she nearly bucked him off, then she turned them—so that he lay flat on his back and she straddled him. He sank deeper than he'd gone before. And his hands, shaking slightly, grabbed her hips.

She rocked back and forth then lifted her hips, sliding his erection in and out of her wet folds. "Julian!" she said, desperation in her raspy voice and dilated eyes.

He moved his fingers to her butt, clasping her soft skin with one hand while he raised his other hand to her breast and massaged the swollen flesh. She lifted her hands to his shoulders, digging her nails in as she rode him.

Her mouth had taken the edge off his urgency, so that he could take his time now, teasing her to the brink of release only to pull out again. Her muscles clutched at him, pulling him deeper. And she knocked his hands aside to cup her breasts and roll her nipples between her thumbs and forefingers. Julian sat up and flicked his tongue across the tips she teased herself. Then he reached between them, sliding his thumb across the most sensitive part of her.

And she came, screaming his name—pouring her passion over him. He dug his fingers into her butt, lifting her up and down, until another orgasm slammed through him—this more violently than the last. "It's a good thing we can't die," he murmured between desperate pants for breath, "or you'd kill me for sure."

She collapsed against his chest, pressing her lips to where his heart pounded hard in rhythm with hers. "I will never hurt you," she promised him.

He smoothed his hands over the perspiration-slick skin of her bare back and asked, "So are you ready to make an honest man of me now?"

Her lips curved against his skin, into a smile. "Honest man?"

"When are you going to marry me?" he asked, urgency rushing through him despite being completely sexually satiated. He couldn't wait for her to become his bride.

"Now too soon?"

"Now is perfect—as perfect as you are." As perfect as their life together promised to be.

Chapter 9

Stars glittered in the night sky as brightly as the lights wound round the boughs of the pine trees lining the park path. Big snowflakes drifted softly out of the darkness, sparkling as they hit the lights and the path. The flakes dropped onto Sienna's face and slid down her cheeks like the tears she fought from falling.

She would not cry. Not when everything was so perfect…and Julian awaited her, standing next to an Underground minister beneath the tallest pine in the park. Clutching tight to Orson Vossimer's arm, Sienna started down the aisle toward her groom. But the elder Vossimer's steps slowed, and he turned to her.

Had he changed his mind? Was she not good enough to be a Vossimer bride?

"No," he answered aloud her unspoken thoughts. "You're perfect. The perfect bride for my grandson— the perfect princess for the Vossimer prince."

"Because he turned me?" She had to know.

The older man shook his head. "Because you love him as he's always deserved to be loved—completely and unselfishly."

"The same way he loves me."

"I see that now," Orson admitted. "I'm sorry…"

"For trying to kill me?"

The older man's handsome face, so eerily similar to Julian's, lifted in the wicked grin his grandson had evidently inherited from him. "Honey, if I'd actually tried, you would be dead. Not *undead*." He covered her hand with his and squeezed. "I may not be the nicest man, but I'm not a killer."

"But you threatened Julian," she reminded him, unwilling to let the man rewrite history. "You told him—"

"I warned him. I suspected how he felt about you. Ever since he'd pulled you from that crash, he'd had an attachment to you. I wanted to test that attachment."

"So it's not a rule that no human can learn of the Underground?"

He sighed. "It's a rule that fortunately hasn't had to be enforced too often."

Just with her parents. She winced, reliving the accident—reliving her loss. But she wasn't afraid of the dark anymore. Or of loving with her whole heart—the way she loved Julian.

"You wanted him to turn me," she realized. "You wanted us to be together?"

"I wanted my grandson to be happy," he said as he turned toward where Julian waited beneath the lit pine tree. "You make him happy."

"And he makes me happy."

The old man nodded, then added with satisfaction, "And your gift would have been wasted on a human."

"Gift?"

"Telepathy, like your grandmother had," he said and admitted, "and I have."

"I don't have telepathy."

"But you know what Julian's thinking."

Right now she knew he was getting impatient, waiting for his grandfather to bring him his bride. Her lips curved into a reassuring smile she hoped he could see. Or at least feel. "Only Julian," she said. "We have a connection."

"Because of your gift," Orson said.

She shook her head. "Because of our love."

"Love…" Orson sighed. "I guess I might actually have to try it for myself."

They started forward on the path, which wound through chairs that had been set up in the park. Members of the Underground, friends of Julian's who had already accepted Sienna, occupied the chairs. One of those was Ingrid.

"Just be careful," she advised the Vossimer king. "Not all love stories end like Julian's and mine."

Happily ever after. She hadn't thought it existed—despite seeing her grandparents' love for each other. And she never would have believed a man such as Julian existed.

"I'm real," he assured her as he took her hand from his grandfather's arm. "And our love is real."

"And eternal."

"You two are skipping ahead on the vows," the Underground minister teased.

"I guess we didn't need you after all," Julian shot back with a wink.

We didn't, Sienna silently agreed. They'd already forever joined their souls.

Julian winked at her, as if he'd read her mind, which he no doubt had. The two of them were one; they didn't need to repeat the minister's vows to seal their union. But they exchanged their promises and rings, a plain gold band for Julian and Nana's diamond for Sienna, so that they could celebrate their love with their friends and family, those dead and those undead.

Breaking away from the passionate kiss that punctuated their wedding ceremony, Sienna smiled and laughed.

"Happy?" Julian asked, his handsome face beaming with his own joy.

"Yes." And so was Nana. Despite her grandmother being dead, Sienna felt her approval shining down upon her as clearly as the stars and the twinkling Christmas lights.

Reading her thoughts again, Julian nodded. "Even Orson's happy for us."

"He loves you," she said and repeated when she felt her new husband's doubts. "He loves you. He just doesn't know how to express it."

"He doesn't know how to *feel* it," Julian scoffed.

"He wants to try," she defended her new relative.

Julian gestured toward where his grandfather stood near the dark-haired vampiress. "I hope he's not going to try with her."

"I don't think so." Orson was too clever to waste his time with someone who couldn't return his feelings. She sighed and admitted, "I feel sorry for Ingrid."

"Why? If she'd had her way, you'd be dead now," Julian reminded her.

Sienna shook her head. "No, if she had her way, she'd be with the man she loves." A twinge of guilt tempered her happiness. "I'm so lucky that I am…"

"We're so lucky," he said, "to have each other."

Music began to play, softly, from a string quartet set up near the Christmas tree. Julian took her hand in his as he wrapped his other arm around her waist and drew her against his body. Then he began to move in time to each sweet chord.

"We are lucky," she agreed.

"And brave," he said.

They had been brave to open up their damaged hearts to love. "Yes," she agreed.

"You were brave to trust me to turn you," he clarified his compliment, "and not kill you."

"Trust had nothing to do with it," she said. "It was love…"

With them, it would always be love.

For all eternity.

* * * * *

UNWRAPPED
Bonnie Vanak

Dear Reader,

Have you ever received a gift you never anticipated—one that fulfilled your wildest dreams?

That's what happens to the vampire hero of "Unwrapped." Banished to his isolated Maine estate, Adrian is given a suspicious Christmas package by six green gremlins dressed as Santa Claus. The gift is Sarah—a lonely Draicon werewolf on the run from enemies wanting her dead, the same enemies Adrian must kill to regain his clan's acceptance.

It will take everything these two have to destroy the killers after Sarah without surrendering to the feelings they both deny. But it's Christmas and magick is in the air. What better magick than the power of love?

I've always believed the best gifts are expressions of the heart. When Adrian and Sarah learn to share their hearts, they receive a gift they will forever cherish.

I hope you enjoy Adrian and Sarah's story in "Unwrapped." I wish all the best for you this holiday season, and a lifetime of love and romance.

Happy reading,

Bonnie

For my mother, who taught me to believe in Christmas magic and miracles. Miss you, Mom. Love you always.

Chapter 1

For the sake of a werewolf, he was risking his life.

Adrian was a vampire. Powerful and fearless, he could move swifter than the eye could blink. But not now. Peeking over the gray ocean's horizon, the rising sun began to sap his enormous energy.

He was doing all this for Sarah. She was a Draicon, werewolves who once used their magick to learn of the earth, who were now hunted by the more powerful Morphs—former Draicon who embraced evil by killing one of their own.

The Morphs shuffled forward on the beach, saliva dripping from their yellowed fangs. Adrian tensed, waiting to see if they would shift to attack. Sarah's enemies could turn into any animal or insect.

A cluster of hooded vampires suddenly glided onto the nearby dunes. Clad in thick robes to protect them against the encroaching dawn, elders from his clan had come to rescue him. But they would not help until Adrian begged. Those were the rules. This was not their war, and he had broken with his clan to fight in it.

Vampires and werewolves can never be allies, his father always warned.

Sarah rushed past him, kicking up eddies of sand. She stabbed the Morphs in the heart with a steel dagger, killing them instantly. The Draicon was a tough little fighter, but he knew she couldn't face her enemies alone. She'd asked Adrian to join her. No one else stood with her—not her pack, her sister or even her own father.

Only two Morphs remained, but where the hell had they gone? Adrian turned around. His heart jumped into his throat as he spied the pair shifting from sea-gulls, assuming their true shapes behind Sarah. Their dark, soulless eyes glowed red. With the last bit of his strength, Adrian sped to Sarah. He pushed her to safety and turned to take her enemy's blows upon his weak-ening body.

Sensing his weakness, a Morph slashed his cheek with its razor-sharp talons. The creature howled in triumph as Adrian collapsed.

A collective hiss of disapproving anger echoed over the dunes. The Morphs turned and saw the vampires. Their shrieks of outraged fear turned into the cries of seagulls as they shifted and flew off.

He'd failed to defeat the enemy. The price would be banishment, if he lived long enough. Through a dazed fog of pain, he struggled to stand. Adrian held out a hand to Sarah. "Help me," he told her.

Her terrified gaze whirled to the vampires. Iridescent sparks filled the air as she shifted. In wolf form, she raced off. Blood trickling down his face blurred his vision as he stared in grief-stricken disbelief. Sarah, the Draicon he secretly adored. Sarah, now leaving him to die.

The ocean's tumultuous waves crashed over his trembling body, saltwater sealing the deep gouges on his face. The sun's cruel rays touched his skin. A scream tore from his throat as he smelled his flesh scorching. Adrian finally pleaded with the vampires for aid. But instead of rescuing him, his family began mocking him in a chorus of singing laughter…

Singing?

Adrian Thorne struggled out of the throes of the dream that had haunted him for the past decade. In the darkness, he opened his eyes and then snatched up a thick burgundy robe and belted it on, marching toward the window. After depressing the button that opened the heavy metal shutters, he swung open the glass panes. Twilight glimmered on the waves crashing against the sweeping, pink granite bluffs below, reflecting the deep rose and crimson hues of a spectacular Maine sunset. Cold wind whistled inside, whipping back his shaggy black hair.

Adrian stared down at the scene on the deck of his two-story mansion. A chorus of green, grinning faces greeted him. Six gremlins dressed in Santa Claus outfits warbled an off-key rendition of "Jingle Bells." Adrian winced and shouted down.

"Are you trying to raise the undead? Do them a favor, let them rest."

"Adrian!" one squealed at him. "Come down and get your Christmas gift."

"Dare I hope it's peace on earth, or at least peace in my house?" he suggested.

As he shut the window, the gremlins belted out a rap song about "peas on earth." Adrian shook his head and scrubbed the day stubble on his jaw. In a few days, elders from his clan would arrive for the winter solstice convocation. Ten years ago, his father, the clan's leader, had banished him until Adrian restored his honor by killing the Morphs that nearly killed him. But Morphs feared a vampire's power and though Adrian had funded numerous efforts to find them, he had failed to do so.

Only Sarah could lead him to her enemy. And she had vanished without a trace.

Downstairs, he went outside onto the wood deck, relishing the harsh winter wind stinging his cheeks. Squealing, the gremlins rushed over, the pom-pom balls on their Santa hats bouncing. The tallest, only four feet, had tinsel dangling from his pointed ears. Six faces beamed at him, showing rows of serrated teeth.

Snark, oldest of the six brothers, thrust a wrapped package at him. "Merry Christmas!"

Adrian felt a small tug of pleasure as he examined the shoebox-size package, his first gift in years. It was wrapped in gold-and-red striped paper that bore faint stains, and the red ribbon smelled like oranges and sour chicken. He raised a dark brow.

"Have you been rooting through the garbage again?"

A chorus of innocent nos with equally innocent looks confirmed his suspicions.

"Open it, open it," they began to chant.

"We got you exactly what you wanted. Just add water and read the note," Snark added.

Curiosity consumed him. He headed for the nearby pool house, the gremlins skipping in his wake. Inside, he switched on the soft overhead lights and sat at the wrought-iron table. Slowly he began to unwrap the present, wanting to make it last. The gremlins squealed with impatience.

Oh, very well. Adrian ripped the paper and tore off the box lid. He lifted a thin layer of tissue paper.

Beneath it lay the ugliest doll he'd ever seen. The smile died on his face. A black, Frankenstein-like scar snaked down the doll's right cheek. Tufts of hair grew from a balding scalp. She was dressed in a lime-green polyester pants suit. A silver bracelet was included in the box, along with a small white card. He read the card. *Congratulations, You are now the proud owner of a Sally Ugly Bunch doll.* There was an 800 number and a Web site address at the bottom.

"Have fun playing with your gift!" Snark chortled, and they scampered off.

A hollow ache filled his chest as he lifted the doll. His fingers stroked the deep gouges on his left cheek. The doll stared sightlessly back at him, its own scar mocking him. Adrian glanced in the direction the gremlins took.

"I thought you were my friends," he whispered.

Grief twisted and writhed like hissing snakes in his

belly. Primitive rage exploded, making his fangs descend. Adrian shook the doll, his voice a strong roar that echoed through the pool house's open glass doors and over the five acres of his cliffside estate.

"Damn you!" He threw the doll against the wall.

"Ouch."

He froze. Were the gremlins playing another trick? Snark said to add water. Adrian picked up his Christmas gift and marched outside. The pool was heated, and remained uncovered for the gremlins' nightly swim. Wind billowed his robe, fluttering it open and exposing his strong, muscled legs. He flung the toy into the water.

Shock filled him as the doll began to thrash. Stiff limbs became arms and legs beating the water. The doll grew to life-size, dark hair sprouting from its balding head. No longer a doll, but a woman.

She sank, only to surface again. "Help me," she choked out, before she went under.

This time she did not surface.

He was no hero. The last time he'd played the part, he'd been left to die. But he was no ogre, either. Shrugging out of his robe, Adrian dove into the pool. He swam underwater, grabbed the woman and dragged her upward. Swiftly towing his gift to the pool's edge, he then climbed out and hoisted the woman up into his arms.

Inside the warm pool house, he gently laid her down on the tiled floor. He inhaled, taking her scent into his lungs. Fangs exploded in his mouth as a familiar hunger seized him.

Only one woman could cause this kind of volatile reaction. Stunned, Adrian took a closer look. The repulsive scar was gone, replaced by smooth flesh. Instead of a chubby moon face, bulbous nose and thin mouth, she had full lips, a pert nose, high cheeks and long lashes.

Shocked, he sat back on his haunches. Adrian bent closer. "My beautiful Sarah," he whispered. "Just as lovely as when you left me. Traitor."

She lay still as cold marble. Very gently, he turned her head to one side. Adrian straddled her hips. Decades ago, he'd given CPR to a little boy who'd nearly drowned. Now he avoided everyone and was dead inside. But maybe he could give life again.

He compressed her chest. She coughed, and a stream of water spilled out of her lips. Satisfaction filled him as color returned to her cheeks. He did another compression and she coughed again.

The delicate blue vein in her throat throbbed with life. Just as he'd always done in the past, he fought the ferocious urge to take her blood. Instead, he stroked her throat, marveling at the feel of satin skin beneath his caressing fingertips.

Blood pulsed just beneath smooth flesh, calling to him in a siren song. He hadn't been near a woman in years, not even to feed. Adrian didn't trust the darkness inside him. His private blood bank took care of his needs.

Clenching his fists, he stared at her lying beneath him. He envisioned Sarah naked, her long legs open, her body sultry and inviting. Flat on her back, the perfect position to sink his fangs, and his body, into her. The strong sexual pull he'd always experienced around her, and never fulfilled, roared to unwelcome life.

Sarah was forbidden. He'd hungered for her, would

have given her the world, but destiny promised her to another of her kind. Adrian had honored her chastity, guarding it from all, even himself. He had never even kissed her.

He could not help himself now. His fangs lengthened, echoing the raw desire pooling much lower. Adrian leaned down, and brushed his mouth against hers. Warm, wet lips moved beneath his. She tasted as delicious as he'd imagined.

Enchanted, he deepened the kiss, moaning at the honey of her mouth. Adrian reluctantly drew away. How the hell had she gotten here? He fetched the note from the doll's box.

"Dear Adreean," (the gremlins had never learned to spell, despite his best efforts to teach them). "Puleze accept with thankz thiz fer letting uz stay on yur guezt houze without pay. We finds her after we smells wolfie when letting air out of car tyers in town. Put thee bracelet on her and she cant do magickz. Meerry Chrismes."

He crushed the note beneath his fingers. Adrian smiled darkly as he retrieved the silver bracelet. He had a pretty Christmas present. And he wasn't about to let her go.

Not until she lured her enemies to his house so he could destroy them and gain admittance back to his clan. Take his rightful role as his father's heir and future ruler of the powerful clan of vampires.

As he snapped the bracelet on her wrist, feeling the chilled, but soft skin beneath his fingertips, he only hoped the old feelings he harbored for her would not destroy him first.

Chapter 2

A naked man had kissed her. The warmth of his wet mouth had spread through her icy body like lava. Making her blood sing, filling her with life.

I'm hallucinating.

Shivering and coughing, Sarah Roberts tried to clear the thick haze in her mind. Her eyes fluttered open. She tried to get a bearing on her surroundings. Her powerful senses picked up distant waves crashing against rocks, the mournful howl of a bitter wind skirting over the cliffs, smelled chlorinated water.

She was wet.

Remembering her pursuers, Sarah bolted upright. She raised her hands to ward off the enemy. A curious draining sensation made her limbs lethargic. Her gaze fell to the circle of silver encasing her right wrist.

Trapped by silver, she couldn't shift or perform magick. Terror and confusion collided together. Sarah fisted her badly shaking hands. They wanted her afraid. The Morphs would feed on her fear as she lay dying. Let them try. She'd go down fighting. A growl rumbled deep in her throat.

"Feisty little thing, aren't you?"

The deep timbre of the sensual voice sounded both familiar and dangerous. She inhaled and a delicious, spicy scent filled her senses, tugging at her memories. This was no Morph. She smelled vampire.

"Who are you?" she demanded.

"Ho, ho, ho."

She knew that voice. From where? Sarah turned. A man sat on a chair, a damp robe clinging to his powerful body. His face was hidden, his body silhouetted by the outdoor lights ringing the pool. The scent of chlorine covered him, as well.

He'd briefly, sweetly, kissed her. No, not a man, but something much more powerful and deadly, someone she knew. Her fingers grasped her wet clothing with growing dismay.

Yuck. Polyester. How did she wind up wearing this?

Then she remembered.

She'd been driving home after visiting distant relatives in Maine in hopes of finding a mate and had been in such a rush that she'd failed to wear the perfume that usually masked her scent. The Morphs picked up her trail. And sensing a vampire nearby, and knowing how

Morphs feared them, Sarah detoured through the tiny seaside town of Anderson. But in town, the aging Ford's transmission finally bought it. A band of gangly Santas cheerfully bearing tools offered help. But instead of Mr. Goodwrench, she got…

Gremlins.

They had been in human form, then shifted into little green headaches. They took the watch from her wrist, chanted something, and she found herself trapped inside a plastic body.

She gingerly touched her temple, recalling the man's warm mouth moving over hers.

"Why did you kiss me?" she accused the silent figure.

"I saved you from drowning." The man stood and hovered over her, his face in shadow. "It's called CPR," he drawled.

He bent over, grasped her hand and pulled her to her feet. Surprised by his strength, she studied her rescuer. The gap in his robe revealed an intriguing triangle of muscled chest. Fascinated, Sarah reached out to run her hand over it.

He stepped back. "Get out of those clothes. I have towels and a warm robe."

Panic raced through her. "I'll just dry off like this." Sarah shook her body, flinging water droplets.

"I would expect as much. You always were very much the wolf." Stray moonbeams glinted off two gleaming fangs as he flashed a humorless smile.

She shivered. But an odd, poignant yearning collided with instinctive caution. The vampire turned his face to the light. Sarah recoiled in startled recognition. Once she'd thought he was the world, then her world changed and everything spun around like a crazy carnival ride.

"Oh, Adrian." Joy filled her as she stepped forward to hug her old friend. "I thought I'd never see you again."

He swept her a courtly bow, his gaze mocking as he straightened. "A valid assumption, Sarah, since the last sight I had of you was of your lovely ass racing away as I was dying. I believe we have a score to settle."

He hadn't forgotten or forgiven. Sarah dropped her arms. "How did you find me?"

"My little green friends are quite adept at flushing out scents, especially wolf, since few Draicon invade my territory." His white teeth gleamed in the moonlight.

"Adrian, you've got to take the bracelet off. The two Morphs that escaped are after me and if they come here, you'll be caught in a very personal, ugly war." Her voice dropped to a pained whisper. "I don't want to do that to you again."

Adrian raised a dark brow. "You're not leaving. Not until you help me settle old business."

He flicked a switch and light flooded the room. Two deep gouges demarcated his cheek.

Sarah smothered a gasp with the back of her hand. "You can't get hurt, you're a vampire." Contrary to human myth, vampires were living, breathing creatures born to their extraordinary powers. Their beauty, swiftness and grace made them deadly enemies.

The sneer on Adrian's mouth became more pronounced. "Do you like the artwork? The sunlight weakened my ability to heal."

Her hand automatically went to her bad leg. "Adrian,

I didn't want to leave you, but your family had arrived. I knew they would rescue you."

A shadow chased across his face. Was it regret? "Did you assume as much? They would not. My clan's code forbade rescuing me after I broke the rules unless I humbled myself by begging for help. So I begged, they saved me and then banished me for a decade. I've been alone, except for the gremlins, my daylight guardians."

"I don't understand your people. Why should you have to beg for help?"

"Because I'm the next in line to lead our clan, and when I break a rule, it holds more consequences than if the others do it. My punishment is greater. The rules were meant for a reason, to keep me safe and separate me from all except our people." Adrian looked as if the confession pained him.

Shock slapped her like a wet towel. "You're Marcus's heir? You never said anything."

"Because I didn't want you to feel intimidated or treat me differently. When you asked for my help, I gave it to you, despite my father's angry objections." Ice coated his voice as he stepped closer. "I never imagined you'd run away when I needed you most."

His warm breath feathered over her chilled skin. "Do you know what it's like for a future leader of the most powerful vampire clan to be defeated by the enemies of another species? To admit a weakness to his family? To cast aside all he is and condemn himself to years of solitude? It's not half as agonizing as feeling your flesh burn until you'll say anything, do anything, to escape the sun."

She could feel the heat of his barely banked rage as if emanating from that very sun, but this heat held an icy blast. Sarah wrapped her arms about herself.

"I didn't realize…"

"I abandoned my family and took the side of a werewolf. I did it all for you, because you asked me."

His voice dropped to a bare whisper. "Once I would have done anything for you."

Her heart stilled. "I called you a couple of days after the battle to see how you were recovering, but the phone was disconnected. And I couldn't risk more than that phone call, much as I wanted to go back to you. It was too dangerous for us."

"I was already gone, banished to Maine, and shunned by all other vampires."

"I'm sorry, Adrian. I never thought it would come to this."

"It has." Icy-blue eyes met hers. "And now you're mine."

A slight shiver skated up her spine at the possessive note in his voice. She had to put distance between them. The Morphs were dangerous, but the feelings she still harbored for this vampire were also lethal.

"Revenge is an asinine motivation," she told him.

"Not revenge, Sarah. Something much more important." His expression hardened. "You're very necessary to me right now. If I can't find and defeat the Morphs who escaped me, I'll be banished for good and never rule the clan after my father steps down."

She closed her eyes against the coolness in his gaze. Once she had basked in the warmth of his presence, cherished their time together as they met in secret. Ignoring stern warnings from their families, they'd formed a close friendship eleven years ago, linked by a common love of old movies, books and engaging discussions about world affairs. Sarah's pack was wary of vampires, and his clan disdained all Draicon.

And then she asked Adrian to fight with her against her enemies because she could not face them alone. Never had she imagined he would pay such a terrible price.

Little could be done about the past. She must focus on the present. Her father was safe for now, entrenched among the human world after she'd phoned him last night. But he'd worry, and track her down if she didn't get home to Connecticut by Christmas. James was blind. Without her, he couldn't go anywhere without resorting to magick. And magick would leave a bright spectral trail for the Morphs to follow, as shiny as gold coins winking in the sunshine.

"If I could have changed things, I'd never ask you to stand with me. But you can't keep me here now."

"You're my Christmas gift. I never return gifts." He circled around her with a vampire's deadly grace and lethal quiet.

Her chest felt hollow as she realized her friend was gone for good. In his place was a dangerous vampire who wanted to use her as he wished. With the bracelet on her wrist stripping her powers, she was helpless against him.

I'll find a way out. She must. Her father depended solely on her.

In the moonlight Adrian's blue eyes gleamed like

lasers. He caught her in one hand beneath her chin. Breath caught in her throat as he studied her face as an artist would study a sculpture in progress. His gaze dropped to the slender curve of her neck.

"Like what you see?" she snapped.

"You'll do nicely." He dropped his hand.

"For what? I warn you, I bite."

A deep chuckle rumbled from his chest. "So do I." He leaned closer. "My bite is better than yours. You wouldn't feel anything, except a slight sting, and then…ecstasy. I make women cry out, even scream before they faint from the pleasure."

Sarah's insides tightened at the thought of his warm mouth pressed against her chilled skin. Kissing his way up her throat, those white fangs sinking into her neck as she clutched him, moaning as he suckled her.

Hunger flared on his face. She waited in breathless anticipation to see if he would finally capitulate to the need driving him each time they were near. But he only snagged a thick terry-cloth robe from a clothes-peg and draped it over her shoulders. "You'll find out soon enough what I want. In the meantime, let's get you into the house and warm."

Chapter 3

Sitting at the kitchen table, Sarah kept her face expressionless. Once his friend, now Adrian's captive. Though she had to admit, it was a beautiful prison.

The mansion was tasteful and welcoming. Brown leather sofas and overstuffed fabric chairs sat before a river rock fireplace in the living room. French doors that opened to the pool deck held a stunning view of the jagged cliffs and moonlit ocean beyond. A recessed bar featured gleaming crystal stemware and a wine rack. Inside a locked glass cabinet was Adrian's rare collection of Revolutionary War muskets and cannonballs. Books were strewn about the coffee table. Seeing the wine and books had given her a pang of nostalgia, remembering the times they'd spent talking about books while sipping the fine vintages Adrian liked to collect.

He'd shown her to a lavish bedroom. Adrian allowed her to shower. Sarah had sighed with pleasure at the luxury of all the hot water she needed. By the time she'd emerged from a bathroom the size of her apartment, she'd seen that her battered suitcase now sat on the plush blue rug. She'd dressed in a cranberry sweater, her one pair of good black corduroy trousers and boots, and went downstairs. The designer jeans, the ones she'd sweated and saved for, were in shreds. Adrian actually looked slightly abashed when she told him.

"I apologize. The gremlins' taste usually runs to Dolce & Gabbana, not Guess."

He offered to purchase another pair. Sarah demurred. Adrian could afford to buy a yacht filled with Guess jeans, but she didn't take handouts.

Sarah now studied her captor. Adrian stood well over six feet, with wide shoulders and a hint of muscle beneath his clothing. In black wool trousers, a black silk shirt and designer loafers, he had an air of elegance and sophistication.

He was breathtakingly handsome. Heavy, dark brows sat over sharp blue eyes. His chin was strong and square, his lips sensual and full. Dark brown hair fell almost to his collar, clipped shorter than when she'd last seen him. The two deep gouges on his left cheek stood out in stark relief. Even the scars did not mar his beauty, but gave him a dangerous look.

Arms folded, Adrian leaned against the Sub-Zero stainless refrigerator.

"Release me, Adrian. I have to get back home, where it's safe."

"Back to your mate? He can't protect you as much as I can."

Arrogant, confident vampire. "I have no pack anymore, and no mate."

His expression remained hooded. "He's out there. You'll find him eventually, as all Draicon do with their destined mates."

"If they're still alive. Mine isn't. My destined mate died long ago."

Was that surprise flaring in his keen gaze? "You were waiting to find him when we were friends. I honored your commitment to mate with him. I never even…"

His voice trailed off, but she knew what he meant. *Never even kissed you.*

She bit her trembling lip, remembering his soft kiss after he'd rescued her from the pool. "He was killed when I was just a child, years before you and I ever met."

Adrian's mouth thinned. "Your father told me he was alive."

"James was afraid of you becoming too friendly with me. Draicon males can scent when another male has been…intimate with a female. And a vampire, well, a vampire is to the Draicon, you know."

"No, I don't know. Why don't you tell me? Lay it out, Sarah. What are we? Enemies?"

Bitterness lashed his voice. He looked as remote as the Arctic.

"You know your clan and my father would never

approve of us," she whispered. "Your own clan pun-
ished you for taking my side. My father warned that
vampires and werewolves can't be friends. Our passions run too high. Family loyalty must come first or
we lose everyone close to us. You and I…"

Words hung unspoken in the air. *We were never
meant to be.*

"I already lost my clan for ten years and high
passions can also make for very pleasant pastimes,
Sarah," he said in a dangerously soft voice.

"Why did you bring me here, Adrian?"

"I've never taken a werewolf before. I hear they are
quite wild in bed."

Tendrils of heat curled through her at the image of
his muscular body naked as he turned to take her into
his arms. Adrian's gaze burned into hers.

"What do you really want?" she asked again, her
heart racing.

"You."

He glided toward her with inborn grace and brack-
eted his arms on the chair, caging her. She breathed in
his masculine scent. Even among all the males of her
kind, none had ever compared to Adrian.

Ice filled his gaze once more. "My clan won't take
me back until I restore my lost honor by defeating the
Morphs I failed to kill. Any efforts I've made to find
them have failed. My clan arrives in a few days for the
convocation at midnight on Christmas Eve when I must
prove I've killed the enemy. I need you to lure the
Morphs here for me."

Real fear replaced rising desire. "I've hidden from

these Morphs for ten years and now you want me to be bait? You must hate me, Adrian."

His gaze softened. "I would never allow them to touch one hair on your pretty head. I'll protect you, Sarah."

"And during the day?" She tried to push away, but he kept a firm grip on her chair.

"The gremlins will watch over you. Their magick is very powerful."

"Oh, sure. They managed to convince me that they could fix my car. That's magick."

His mouth crooked up in a charming grin. "They did fix your car instead of eating the engine. I'd say that was very good magick."

The grin stilled her. She saw the old Adrian, full of mischief and fun. For a moment, time slid back. How she wished she could have told him the full truth when she pleaded for his help that night on the shore.

Regrets were a waste of time. "You don't seem to understand. These Morphs will stop at nothing until I'm dead."

"Why do they want you so much, Sarah? There's a host of other Draicon out there to feed off. What is it about you they crave?"

Raising her chin, she met his hard look with a brave one. "James and I are on our own. We're packless, and more vulnerable because we have no one to stand with us against an attack."

"What happened to your mother and sister?"

Tears burned in her throat. "Dead, that day you and I fought on the beach. My father and I ended up running for our lives."

He looked stunned. "I'm sorry, Sarah. How did it happen?"

"An unexpected enemy killed them."

Adrian pulled out a chair, sat beside her. His gaze sharpened even as he held her hand in a comforting gesture. "That day we fought on the beach, you said you needed my help because your pack was protecting your mother. She was pregnant with the heir, and your sister and father stayed behind to guard her, as well. So what happened? Where's your pack?"

She said nothing.

"Tell me."

His voice carried a hint of command, layered with a vampire's natural enthrallment. Sarah fought against it.

"They scattered. It's a moot point, okay? What's important is the Morphs after me will destroy anything and everything that stands in their way."

He leaned closer, so close she could count the bristles shadowing his hard jaw. "Bring them on. I'll defeat them for you, win back my clan's approval. No Morph can best me."

Power shimmered in the air. She didn't doubt he could take on a legion of them without breaking a sweat. The ones he'd battled would never have scratched him, if not for the rising sun.

The Morphs could take her life. But Adrian could take her heart, and then shatter it like glass. She'd spent the past decade picking up the shards of her former life. Hadn't she already endured enough?

Sarah pushed away from the table. He blocked her way. Adrian's long fingers gently caught her wrist.

"You will stay here." His thumb stroked over her skin, creating a flare of pulsing desire. "I'll keep you safe, Sarah."

His touch soothed her. For a moment she wanted to stop running, and fall into his arms. Sarah pulled away from the temptation. Never would she allow anyone to draw close. There was no one she could trust, especially not Adrian.

His eyes grew brilliant as he watched her. White ringed the blue irises, as if they shimmered with light.

"The Morphs who are after me have learned a few tricks. I can't stay here."

Adrian released her wrist. "I've learned a few tricks, as well. And so have you, to evade them, and me, all these years. Why did you run away from me, Sarah? Such a mystery. I will find out why."

She hid a wince as cramps tightened her left leg. Sarah drew in a deep breath, working past the pain. Shoulders squared, she studied her captor.

"If you're done with the inquisition, I'd like to go to bed."

A slow smile touched his mouth. "Do you?"

Her heart gave a funny little jerk. "Maybe I'll settle for a walk on the beach," she muttered.

Adrian raised a dark brow. "It's cold on the shore."

Not as cold as it is in here. "I'll survive." She gestured to carving knives on the counter. "Those steel?"

Adrian nodded.

Gritting her teeth against the pain of her bad leg, she tried to walk normally to examine the blades. But it proved impossible. Her left leg pulled like a lead weight.

A frown touched his face. "Did I hurt you when I threw you into the pool?"

"You can't hurt me," she shot back. "I'm tougher than that silly doll."

"I don't doubt it."

She selected two knives, slid both through her belt. Adrian watched.

"Since when do you arm yourself to walk on the beach?"

Her chest felt compressed. "Since my old life went to hell. But you wouldn't know anything about what that's like."

"Hell isn't reserved exclusively for Draicon," he said quietly.

Arms folded, he looked down at her, power surrounding him like a dark cloak. Sarah's heart gave a little lurch. She dared to place her hand on his arm, feeling the tensile muscles tighten.

His eyes darkened. Then Adrian jerked free of her touch and walked away. Just as she had walked away from him years ago. At the doorway, he paused and spoke over his shoulder.

"Take my coat from the hall closet."

Warmth surrounded her as she shrugged into Adrian's fur-lined black cashmere coat. She almost moaned in delight from the toasty feeling, the delicious scent that was uniquely his.

A cold ocean breeze whipped at her hair as she went outside. Pebbles crunched beneath her boots as she followed the pathway down the cliff to the sandy beach. Craggy cliffs, laced with outcroppings of pink granite, stood as a silent sentinel over the horseshoe-shaped bay.

Sarah watched the white froth of angry ocean waves. Salty spray stung her cheeks, but the briny air rejuvenated her. She and James had lived in urban centers, avoiding the pricier areas they couldn't afford.

After years of hiding, she and her father had finally settled, found jobs and had a little money. Their savings wouldn't even cover one month of Adrian's electric bill, but it was theirs. Now, thanks to her expedition to find a mate for herself and a pack for her father, they'd been discovered by the enemy. All for nothing. Her distant cousin Cameron hadn't wanted her any more than the other males she'd sought out.

Oh, the pack had been friendly and Terrence and Elaine, the alpha couple, couldn't have been nicer. Cameron even liked her. But then her cousin had "accidentally" caught sight of her as she emerged from the shower. The towel had covered all essential parts, except her legs. The shock on Cameron's face had quickly turned to revulsion. He'd left the house, leaving his parents puzzled and asking questions she didn't want to answer. Filled with shame, she'd given polite excuses and left.

Relishing the stinging spray on her face, Sarah began to hunt for sea glass. The simple pleasure washed away the hurt of Cameron's rejection, the uncertainty about being Adrian's captive. Something in the water caught her eye. Fish, jumping and leaping in the water, grayish moonlight glinting off their silvery scales. Suddenly the water began to churn.

Sarah backed off instinctively, drawing closer to the

cliffs. The boiling mass in the ocean swam closer. Her blood ran cold as an explosion of white, sightless crabs spilled onto the shore.

Morphs.

Don't panic. She forced concentration, dragged in their scent. Morphs could mask their scent, but a skilled Draicon could detect a faint trace of their original packs. These were clones. Not as powerful, but still deadly. Oh, sweet mercy, they were coming after her.

Do something!

Sarah ran. She could hear them closing up behind her, their claws eager to snap at her flesh. Panic squeezed her throat. She forced it down, whirled. Both knives came out with practiced ease. *See them as they really are, they're evil, they're killers.*

Thoughts of Adrian loaned her strength as she remembered how he'd fearlessly engaged them. Shoulders thrown back, she screamed, "You can't do this to me anymore. Come on and fight me, bastards."

The mass of Morphs shape-shifted. Nausea boiled in her stomach.

"Oh, rats," she muttered.

A mass of dark rodents streamed toward her. Holding out the knives, she stood ready to pounce. They ground to a halt a few feet away. Dark power shimmered in the air as a rat shifted to a human form. A sob wrenched her throat.

It was a clone, an exact imitation of someone who'd loved her. The one person she'd sworn to never, ever forsake.

"Sarah," it whispered into the night wind.

It shifted again, the face contorting, body twisting. Sarah lowered her weapons.

"Why?" she asked brokenly.

Something rushed past her like a spinning tornado. She caught Adrian's tangy scent. In helpless anguish, she stood as if her feet were nailed to the pebbled sand. Movement blurred the air as the vampire killed the Morphs. One shifted into its true form, a hunched creature with yellow fangs, a red, wet twist of a mouth yawning wide-open.

In the blink of an eye, Adrian stabbed it in the heart. The Morph gave a dying shriek and dissolved into thick, gray ash.

Wind spun the dust of her dead enemies into a cloud. Something was clattering violently. Her teeth.

Adrian glided over, clasped her wrists, making her drop the knives. He gently rubbed her arms. "Are you all right? Did they hurt you?"

She shook her head.

"Sarah, why didn't you defend yourself?"

Wordlessly, she stared downward. Shame covered her like a wet blanket of fog. She could not voice her darkest fear. Not to him.

He pulled her against his muscular chest.

She collapsed against him, cherishing the feel of his arms drawing tightly around her. For the first time in years, she felt safe. He stroked her hair, each caress a soothing rhythm that settled her raging nerves.

Adrian rested his forehead against hers. "I told you I could handle them," he murmured. "You have nothing to fear."

Letting him this close was dangerous. He could break her heart and it would hurt worse than a thousand lacerations from a legion of Morphs. Sarah jerked away. "Yes, I do." *You.*

Wearily, she pushed back the hair from her face. "These were scouts, flushing out my scent. The original is hiding in the shadows, waiting to amass any weaknesses in your territory before it attacks."

Damn, she was tired. No sustenance since she'd left Terrence's pack. Combined with the silver bracelet draining her energy, she felt ready to drop.

As she turned to leave, her bad leg seized up. Stifling a cry, she pitched forward as her vision went gray.

Chapter 4

Adrian swore a low oath. Lifting her in his arms, he carried her into the living room. Her soft body felt good cradled against him. He laid her on one of the leather couches.

Her complexion was too pale, her cheeks looked slightly sunken. She needed food.

Covering her with a forest-green throw, he returned to the kitchen. Adrian opened the refrigerator. Nothing. There was a thick steak in the freezer. He placed it in the microwave.

While waiting for the beef to defrost, he perched on the sofa. Long, dark eyelashes brushed against the pale hollows of her cheeks. Her rosebud mouth was slightly open. Adrian stroked hair away from her face. When had she grown so thin and pale? The Sarah he knew was healthy, curvy and filled with laughter.

Pulled irresistibly by desire, he leaned close. He, the vampire who could have any female in his bed, had not taken a lover since the day Sarah walked into his life. She had waltzed in and stolen his heart as easily as she'd captured his friendship. Eleven years ago Sarah had boldly ignored the dividing lines between vampire and Draicon. She'd knocked on the door of his North Carolina beach home, asking for permission to hunt on his private lands during the full moon. Deeply curious about the lovely Draicon, Adrian had granted it, and had spent the night watching Sarah chase prey and then frolic in the churning, silver-splashed surf. When she'd shape-shifted back into her human form and thanked him, they'd started joking together about old, campy Hollywood vampire and werewolf films.

The microwave dinged, interrupting his thoughts. A few minutes later he carried a plate of rare roast beef to the living room. He waved it beneath her nose.

"Wake up, Sarah. You need food."

Slowly she opened her eyes and sat. Her nostrils flared as she saw the fresh meat.

Adrian sensed her deep pride fighting with the ravenous hunger. He set the plate down on the coffee table and walked to the window.

Soon as he did, he heard her quietly gulp down the meal. His heart ached. When had she last eaten? What the hell had become of her?

Why should he care? He hated to admit he still did.

He could not afford to care. After dispatching her

enemy, he must send her on her way. Arms folded, he stared into the darkness. Any desire he had for Sarah must be controlled. Adrian was his father's heir, and no one would stand between him and his clan ever again.

Adrian studied the shadows. He spoke over his shoulder. "I'll place safeguards around the property to protect you."

"They'll find a way inside. Even your powers can't stop them."

His temper flared at the insinuation he was weak, but he held his anger. "I doubt it. You have no idea of the full extent of my powers," he murmured. "But it's obvious they've grown stronger. The new tricks they learned include cloning themselves and shifting faster."

"They prefer attacking as wolves, the original Draicon form. Takes less energy. They shift into their true Morph form to feed."

"I remember that. What else should I expect?"

The plate clanked down. "Everything. Everything beyond your darkest dreams, your worst nightmares." She added quietly, "Or mine."

Something inside him twisted at her pain. He wanted to pull her into his sheltering embrace, let her rest there. Eradicate everything she'd felt the past years, and restore the wide smile she'd once always worn. Fisting his hands, he steeled himself against the temptation. But he must know why she abandoned him.

Adrian sat beside her on the sofa. "Why did you leave me, Sarah? Was it to save your own skin? Tell me."

Damn, he hated to use his enthrallment, the command

in his voice no one, not even a stubborn Draicon, could resist. But he must find out, so they both could move on.

"Never. I would have died with you. I had to get home, save her."

"Save who, Sarah?" he demanded.

"I knew what was happening, I was stupid, ignored the danger signals, I didn't want to believe it…my mother, screaming…"

The sob wrenched from her throat stabbed his heart. He waved a hand before her face. "Hush," he soothed. "You will sleep tonight, sleep well and remember only pleasant memories."

She blinked. Her hand slid over his, the warmth of her skin flooding him with the need to touch her further. Adrian stared down at her fingers encircling his. He lifted her work-scarred knuckles and kissed each one.

Contact sizzled between them. A fierce longing seized him. Couldn't help the wanting, the deep need to bury his body and his fangs deep inside her, so deep she could never get rid of him, would always carry his scent, the imprint of his passion. He wanted all of her, the Sarah who had laughed with him, bravely faced her enemies, the woman whose laughter sounded like the pealing of tiny silver Christmas bells.

He could not have her. Adrian dropped her hand.

"Go to bed," he said, retreating back to the window.

"I never like to be in debt to anyone," she told him. "If I'm to stay here, then I insist on paying my way."

Adrian turned and studied her clean but threadbare clothing, her slender shoulders stiff with dignity. Sarah could not pay him. But he knew well the importance of maintaining one's pride.

"Take charge of the delivery of fresh blood tomorrow from my private blood bank and stock the refrigerator. When I rise, have a bottle warmed and ready. That will suffice for payment."

As he heard her murmur good-night, he did not voice the other payment his heart longed for with all his might.

And kiss me, Sarah. Kiss me and let me hold you in my arms, and shut away the weary world.

Chapter 5

Sarah snapped awake in the darkness. The digital clock on the nightstand read 3:00 p.m. She switched on a lamp. Adrian had shuttered the windows against the glaring sunlight.

Last night, she'd called her father, trying to reassure him all was well and she'd experienced a slight delay. But he didn't buy it. If she weren't home two days before Christmas, he would fetch her himself.

A shower cleared her muzzy head. Afterward, she sorted through her battered suitcase for fresh clothing, selecting a powder-blue turtleneck and faded jeans.

Except she couldn't find her good bra.

A loud thud sounded. Outside, someone was having target practice.

She went downstairs.

Sunlight beamed through the mansion's lower floor. Adrian had thoughtfully left all the shutters open, either for her or his gremlin friends. She peered through the French doors.

Her heart went still, then anger raced through her. Sarah grabbed her worn sheepskin jacket and raced outside. Her breath fogged the crisp winter air. Ice crystals formed on overhanging tree limbs. New snow blanketed the grounds, the brightness of the day nearly hurting her eyes.

"Hey, stop it!"

With military precision, the six green gremlins had lined up Adrian's antique cannonballs. In the distance was a dummy. Two gremlins stretched out her white garment on either side, as a third placed two cannonballs inside. A fourth pulled it back like a slingshot.

"Incoming!" the gremlin bellowed, sending the balls flying toward the dummy.

They were using her bra as a launcher. Her one good bra she'd bought in a half-price sale at Macy's.

Sarah raced forward, snatched it from their startled grasp. "That's mine," she snapped.

"We's need it for target practice," the shortest protested. "It was the only thing that fit the ammo."

"Get your own," she grated out, staring in dismay at the stretched garment. Rust smeared the pretty white satin.

"In any war, there's sacrifices," the tallest stated. He peered up at her. "Adrian said there was a battle, and we's should prepare to remove the heads of the enemy."

Sarah wished she could take off their heads. "By

fighting with my bra. Oh, that's rich. Adrian said your magick was powerful. I'd be better off guarded by the Three Stooges."

White sparks of power filled the air, nearly knocking her off her feet. Her gaze swiveled to the target. She stared at the smashed dummy, blown to bits by the burst of energy zinging from the gremlin's fingertips.

"Then again," she murmured.

The tallest gremlin blew at his index finger as if it were a smoking pistol. He extended a green palm toward her. "Introductions are necessary. Our mother always said we's shouldn't act as if we's was raised in a barn…"

"Even though we's were," another chimed in.

She shook the proffered hands. Snark was the tallest, followed by his brothers, Trip, Grimace, Wedgie, Short and the smallest was 404.

"Named after the computer error message," 404 told her.

Wedgie grinned, showing rows of pointed teeth. "Adrian said last night you had a bad case of crabs."

Laughter bubbled up in her chest. She tossed the bra back at them. "Here. I have another. Besides, it's ruined now. One question. Why did you dress me in polyester when you turned me into a doll?"

Grimace looked surprised. "We's thought it would drain your magick. We's used gloves, because it drains our magick. We's terrified of it."

"Makes sense," she murmured. "It scares me, too."

She glanced at the gray shingled home, sitting on the cliffs in aloof splendor as it overlooked a gray sea. Soon it would be turned into a battle zone. Her chest felt hollow with regret as she thought of Adrian dying on the beach, his clan silently waiting for him to call for help.

If I had only known....

Sarah turned her face to the sun. Light was her friend, for Morphs couldn't use the shadows to hide. It was Adrian's enemy, and had burned his flesh. If only she could take back that day.

When she went inside, the gremlins followed. She looked at them. "What are you doing?"

Trip looked surprised. "We keep Adrian's home safe during the day and Adrian told us to make sure to guard you, as well."

His edict touched her. No one had seen to her needs in a long time.

No one would again, after Adrian released her. As Sarah shrugged out of her jacket, a soft chime at the front door reminded her of the promise she'd made. After signing for the collection of blood, she unpacked the cold case and stocked the bottles in Adrian's glass wine refrigerator.

The gremlins watched in silence. She turned to them. "How did you know it was me when you were in town?"

Snark looked impish. "Come with us."

They led her to a dark study upstairs, switched on an overhead light. A massive mahogany desk and matching credenza dominated the room. On the desk sat an LCD computer screen.

"Adrian's computer. He keeps tabs on all his businesses from here," Short told her.

Grimace slid into the black leather chair, pushed a button on a slim tower sitting beneath the desk. The gremlin shot his brother an accusing look. "404, have you been playing games on the computer again?" He pointed to the blue screen.

"Oops," came the reply.

Snark sniffed. "Short, nothing more."

Short went beneath the desk, fiddled with cables. "This may take a few minutes."

The clock indicated it was nearly sunset. Adrian would soon rise and be hungry. While the gremlins worked on the computer, Sarah fetched a bottle of blood. She warmed it in the kitchen and placed it on the counter for Adrian.

When she returned to the study, the computer was finally powering up. Grimace tapped a few keys. "This is how we knew who you were," he told her as the computer kicked into screen-saver mode.

Breath fled her lungs.

A face stared at her from the screen. A face she barely recognized, molded into a laugh, eyes sparkling with life, the dark hair shining in the sun's setting rays. Beneath the photo was a caption: *Sarah Roberts, sunset on the beach.*

Adrian put her photo on the computer.

Sarah's finger traced the digitized cheek. Had she been that happy? She'd forgotten.

Adrian had not.

404 peered at the screen. "Where is this?"

"North Carolina. We were walking on the shore. Adrian insisted on testing his new camera. He said I was more photogenic than…"

"The prettiest sunset."

The deep velvet voice came from the doorway. She turned. Fascination stole over her as she realized Adrian wore only black silk pajama bottoms. Never before had he exposed to her so much luscious, tanned skin. Broad, sculpted shoulders rippled with muscles. Muscles ridged his flat abdomen. She stared in fascination at his smooth chest, wondering what it would feel like beneath her exploring fingertips.

Her gaze flicked up, saw him studying her with dark intensity. She turned away, feeling heat flare on her cheeks.

"Your dinner, or breakfast, is in the kitchen," she mumbled.

But he went to her, gently snagged her wrist. "Come with me. I hate to eat alone."

She followed him to the kitchen. Adrian grabbed the bottle of blood, poured a glass and drank. Sarah watched in fascination as his throat muscles worked.

Suddenly he spewed out the contents. "Warm, unsweetened cherry Kool-Aid!" He gagged.

"I filled the bottle with blood just as you asked!" Sarah tensed, expecting him to yell.

Stunned, she watched him wipe his mouth with the back of his hand, throw back his head and laugh. Her appreciative gaze hungrily drank in his powerfully muscled body, the smooth firmness of his chest, the black satin pajama bottoms clinging to his long, athletic limbs.

Filled with amusement, those sunny blue eyes glanced at her. "The gremlins. I should have known. They've done this before, and I told them they would never pull this one on me again. They can't resist a challenge."

"Put a lock on the refrigerator," she suggested.

"Tried that. They ate the lock. Said it was delicious."

Together they burst into laughter. When they finally ceased, Sarah felt wistful for the emotional connection they'd shared—the vampire and the werewolf who liked to watch old movies and discuss books and theater.

When she asked if he worried about the gremlins, he grew serious.

"I took their blood, so I could track them. If one of them were dying, I'd instantly know it. I do it for everyone I care for, including my father, except I was required to take his blood. If my father dies, I instantly sense it and know I must assume leadership to keep the order."

"Why didn't you ever take my blood?" she asked.

He gave her an intent look. "I honored you too much, Sarah. If I took your blood, it would lead…to other things."

He'd never touched her. Adrian's sense of honor had guarded her chasteness.

To hell with honor, she thought suddenly. *Does he want me?*

The same funny flip of her heart happened again, this time combined with a powerful erotic tingling. Her gaze roved over the firm muscle and sinew of his body, the carved planes of his face, the sensuality of his full mouth. His dark brown hair was rumpled. Sarah started to lift her hands to run them through the soft strands.

Clenching her fists, she gritted her teeth. Survival and desire were not good companions.

But she wanted to push him downward, climb over

him, run her tongue over that firm, smooth skin, taste him…

An intent look replaced his amused one. Adrian closed the distance between them. His long, tapered fingers slid around her neck, caressing the bare skin beneath the fall of her hair. Sarah's body tightened with each slow stroke.

He pulled her toward him, his mouth lowering on hers. Sarah slid her arms around his neck, closing her eyes. Feelings surged through her at the languid way he kissed her. He deepened the kiss, coaxing her mouth to open beneath the insistent pressure of his.

His hand went to her breast, cupping the heavy weight, his thumb stroking over her hardening nipple. Sarah whispered encouragement as he touched her, each flick of his thumb making her blood run hotter, her body ache with ceaseless yearning.

When she reached behind him and cupped his taut buttocks, he shuddered with pleasure and broke the kiss.

Adrian nuzzled her neck, his hot breath feathering over her skin. He cupped her bottom, lifted her up against the cold steel of the refrigerator. He nudged her legs open, and stepped between them as she wrapped her thighs around his hips. Sarah arched against him, feeling the steely length in his groin. He lifted her so the opened juncture between her legs was centered against his hardness. Sarah dug her nails into his shoulders, tasted the tangy saltiness of his collarbone as she licked his flesh. She rubbed herself against him, gasping with pleasure, hearing him softly encouraging her to let go, surrender to it….

The feelings built to a crescendo, and with a tiny cry

she let go. Her head hung back limply, sweat dampening her temples as she gasped for air.

Slowly he lowered her trembling body to the floor, his gaze burning into hers. Sarah ran a hand down his front, gliding over his flat abdomen, down to the silkiness of his pajama bottoms and his thick erection. She stroked through the thin covering, watching his heavy-lidded gaze darken.

Adrian growled deep in his throat, lowering his head to the vulnerable curve of her neck. She felt the erotic brush of his lips nuzzling her tender flesh, then the intriguing, sharp rasp of his fangs gently scraping her skin.

Ready to pierce, take her blood, marking her as his exclusively.

Reason returned like a hard slap to her cheek. Sarah jerked away, startling him. The dark intent in his eyes flared again as he regarded her.

"This is crazy," she muttered, holding her hands out as if to stop him. As if she could stop him, this powerful vampire accustomed to getting anything he wanted. In her weakened state, he could topple her with the flick of a finger. He could take her blood, those long fangs sliding into her flesh and she couldn't stop him, wouldn't have the strength.

Or the will.

"I can't do this. I'm still untouched, understand, Adrian? I'm a virgin because I need a mate of my own kind willing to take me in and that's all I have to offer. I can't go to another male marked by the scent of a vampire who took me and my blood."

"Sarah, look at me," he said quietly.

She didn't want the enthrallment in his eyes to spell-bind her. But the command in his tone made her lift her helpless gaze.

Hands clenched into trembling fists at his sides, he studied her. The haunted look on his face twisted her heart. She wanted to wrap her arms about him and never let go and give in to the passion they both shared.

It wasn't possible.

"I will never, ever, do anything to hurt you. Do you understand? Even to the extent that it might hurt me. I will never do anything you don't want me to."

Slowly she relaxed, but his body tensed even more. He jammed a hand through his mussed hair. Something she couldn't read flickered in his eyes.

"Have dinner with me. Tomorrow night." His mouth twisted up in a mocking smile. "I promise I won't bite. Please."

Sarah nodded, leaving the room. Won't bite. She could trust he wouldn't.

But never trust herself not to want it.

Chapter 6

The gremlins were having trouble with the Christmas tree.

All six struggled to straighten the seven-foot balsam pine delivered that afternoon. Fresh pine tickled her senses. Sarah smiled as she unpacked the boxes of decorations. She'd seen little of Adrian last night, as he had a meeting in town. Now she enjoyed watching the little green monsters try to best the tree. The tree was winning.

"It's crooked," she teased them.

"We's know that," Wedgie said. "We's just trying to decide what to use to anchor it to the wall so it's straight."

"Sometimes whatever you have on hand works best," she replied, and went upstairs to change for dinner.

An elegant, floor-length red dress was laid out on the

bed. Sarah picked up the garment, stroking the red velvet designer dress. Two diamond clasps were at the shoulders, the bodice was a deep V. She spotted a note in Adrian's firm, bold handwriting.

"Please indulge me and wear this tonight. The shoes are in the closet."

Clutching the treasure, Sarah padded over to the room-size closet.

On the floor were red Jimmy Choo shoes. They fit perfectly. A smile touched her mouth as she headed into the shower.

Her cell chirped softly. Sarah's heart sank when she saw the number. Terrence. Probably questioning her hasty departure. She answered it.

The startling conversation that followed filled her with joy and hope. When she closed the phone, she studied the bracelet holding her captive.

"Distant cousins or not, you and your father are family," the alpha male had told her. "Cameron admitted what happened. He's ashamed and wants to apologize. My mate and I would be honored if you and your father would join our pack. We'll help you defeat your enemies, honey. Draicon must stick together."

Draicon needed to stick together. Not Draicon and vampires. She could finally bring her father to a pack that wanted them.

Sarah fiddled with the silver binding on her left wrist. It was looser. The gremlins had made one mistake in fashioning the magick handcuff. They'd failed to take into account that the metal shrank in the cold outdoors, but would expand inside the warm house.

She tugged harder, succeeding in inching it a quarter of the way down her hand. Sarah stared at the bracelet. She was strong enough to yank it off now, if she risked the pain. Escape was in her grasp.

With trembling hands, she stroked the soft red velvet. One dinner with Adrian surely could not hurt. She had tonight. Tonight must be enough.

Even though in her heart she knew it could never be enough.

Sarah dressed carefully, pulling white silk stockings over her long legs, enjoying the swish of heavy velvet as it cascaded to her ankles.

The image staring at her in the mirror was stunning. Sarah touched the glass, hardly able to believe it was her. "I look pretty," she murmured.

Jazz played softly in the background as she went downstairs. In the dining room a polished walnut table was set with china, sparkling crystal and heavy silver. A setting of red poinsettias and fresh holly adorned the center. But it was Adrian, clad in a black designer dinner suit with a white starched tie and pearl-buttoned shirt, who made her breath catch.

She murmured a compliment, gratified at the admiration in his own eyes. "You're so beautiful," he said in a husky voice.

Her hand lovingly caressed the red velvet. "Your favorite color."

A roguish grin touched his full mouth. "The color of passion."

The same color tinted her cheeks. Adrian's smile deepened. He held out her chair, but instead of pushing it in, easily lifted the chair with her in it to the table. Sarah turned with a teasing look.

"Show-off."

"Always," he murmured, and they laughed.

He expertly uncorked a bottle of wine and sampled it. He poured her a glass. They sipped the vintage. Sarah sighed with pleasure.

"You always did appreciate the finer things in life," he noted.

More so now than before, since I have no money, she thought. But she wouldn't let even that gloomy thought ruin the splendid evening. She raised her glass.

"To Rick," she offered.

His dark, heavy brows knitted together until comprehension dawned on his handsome face. "Ah yes, *Casablanca.*" He looked boyish suddenly as they clinked glasses. "We'll always have Paris."

Sarah drank and set her glass down. "I always wonder whatever became of him. Did he ever find happiness after the war, after letting go of his one true love?"

A mask dropped over Adrian's face. He toyed with the stem of his glass. "Maybe he couldn't let go emotionally, but kept her guarded in his heart, like a secret never shared with the world."

She didn't know how to respond to that.

Dinner was rare prime rib. Sarah ate heartily as Adrian drank from a crystal goblet filled with dark crimson liquid. She gestured to it.

"Did you put a new lock on the fridge?"

"No, I simply warned them if they tampered with my food supply anymore, no more Friday night DVDs."

"The gremlins like to watch DVDs?"

"Not watch. Eat," he replied.

They laughed again.

He leaned forward, reaching out for her hand. "I've missed your smile, Sarah."

Her hand trembled in his. Adrian stroked a thumb slowly over her wrist, the burning intensity of his gaze filled with sexual promise. Her nostrils flared as she caught his delicious, woodsy scent. She studied the hardness of his body, wondering what his muscled weight would feel like lying atop her as he pushed inside her. Moisture trickled between her legs, preparing her flesh for him. She wanted him with a hot, insane need.

Sarah withdrew her hand.

"I need to tell you. The pack I visited, the alpha called and they want to take in my father and me. When I leave here, I'll have a family again."

His expression quickly shuttered. "I'm pleased for you."

But he sounded distant, as if her news was an un-welcome reminder of the barriers sharply dividing their worlds.

They finished eating. Adrian led her into the living room. A window was cracked open, allowing in the cold ocean breeze. Glittering with gold garland, colored lights and brightly colored balls, the Christmas tree stood in a corner. Sarah walked over to it, murmuring with pleasure.

"I wonder how they got it to stay upright."

A small, teasing smile touched the corners of Adrian's mouth. "Look in the back."

She did. Sarah stared at the white, rust-stained garment tied to the tree and nailed to the wall. Her bra.

"They needed something rather large and supportive." This time he chuckled openly and she went to mock-punch him.

He caught her wrists as the music system began playing a sultry jazz tune. His playful expression turned serious. "Dance with me, Sarah."

So few indulgences she'd enjoyed. For once, she threw caution to the wind. One dance. All she had was tonight, and Adrian's own special brand of magick.

She went into his arms. He held her tight as she rested her head against his broad shoulder. Adrian guided her around the room, humming into her ear. Each shift of his body pressed his hard muscles against her softness. It felt good, so right, as if she belonged here. He rocked against her, eradicating everything but the thought of him. If only the night were endless, and the hours would never cease.

All too soon, they would. And soon she would leave him once more.

"The night I fled the beach, I whispered a promise to you." Sarah's throat tightened with the admission. "You were my only friend, Adrian, and it broke my heart to never see you again. So as I ran away, I promised I'd come back to you someday."

He stilled, his expression filled with tenderness. "I never stopped looking for you. Needing to lure in your enemies was an excuse. It was you I searched for all these years, Sarah."

When his lips captured hers, she sighed into his mouth. It was here and right, this moment, living only for the passion of his kiss. Adrian cupped the back of her head, tunneling his fingers through her silky hair. He kissed her with an urgent desperation, as if he never wanted to let her go.

As she kissed him back, she remembered he would have to release her. Their people despised each other. Adrian was needed as his clan's future leader. A Draicon like her, especially a crippled one that no man wanted, could never fit into his world.

All too soon he broke the kiss. Torment filled his gaze as Adrian solemnly regarded her. She put a finger to his warm, wet mouth. "Don't say a word. Just dance with me, for every moment we have left."

They resumed dancing, Sarah resting her head against him. She breathed deeply, taking in his delicious masculine scent of pine and forest, mixing with a faint, odd fragrance of…fruity cologne.

A familiar tingling ran down her spine. She only experienced it when a certain Morph was present. Sarah wrenched away and ran to the French doors.

He was right behind her. "What is it?"

"They're out there."

Adrian frowned. "I can't scent them."

"They've learned to disguise their scent. I've discovered how to detect it. The Morphs last night were sent in to assess weaknesses and find their prey. Now that they know I'm here…"

Her voice trailed off. "But how could they track me so fast, especially since you killed all the ones last night?"

Adrian studied her with a calm look. Suddenly she knew.

"You let a couple escape to bring the others straight to me. Adrian, how could you?"

"I did what I must. The safeguards around the property will protect you."

"And I warned you they can find a way past your damn safeguards. Killing them is everything, isn't it? And here I thought I mattered." She clenched her fists. "You'll do anything to get your justice, and you don't care who stands between you and them. Even me."

"Not true, Sarah." He folded his arms across his chest. "But why have you spent the past ten years running away instead of confronting them? You're a fighter."

"I'm not running now. I'm going out there to face them, even if they kill me."

"Dammit, why won't you tell me what's really going on?" He pushed forward, crowding her until she was pressed against the glass doors. "Don't you trust in my ability to defeat them? I told you I'd never let them hurt you."

"It's not that. I have to do this alone."

His gaze sharpened. "Why, when before, we faced them together?"

"Because there's one Morph I must find the courage to face by myself." She slipped beneath his grasp.

"Where are you going?" he demanded.

"Upstairs to change. Then outside, to do what I couldn't do ten years ago."

When would Sarah trust him? Adrian wondered.

He sped outside into the cold, bitter air. Adrian

loosened his tie, dragged in a lungful of air, smelled nothing. Even his adroit senses could not pick them out.

But Sarah could. She had spent years learning about them, fleeing from them. It was quite possible they could break past his defenses.

He couldn't let her rush headlong into danger. *Even though you placed her in it,* his conscience nagged.

Minutes later, dressed in old jeans, a faded Steelers T-shirt and her sheepskin jacket, she burst out onto the deck. Adrian snagged her about the waist.

"I have to show I'm not afraid," she shouted, struggling to release herself. "Let me go."

"Why now, Sarah?" His arms anchored her to him. She possessed the strength of her kind, but he was far stronger.

"Because I can't run anymore, I have to make a stand."

"Just like you did on the beach? When you trusted me to stand with you?"

Her struggles ceased. Dark eyes wide in her face, Sarah stared at him with a woebegone expression. Adrian's heart lurched. "Sarah, together we can defeat them. You can't fight them alone."

"I have no choice," she whispered brokenly. "This is my problem. My war."

"No, you made it my problem and my war the day you asked for my help."

Her gaze grew flat. She inhaled deeply. "The scent's gone. They're gone."

They went back inside. Adrian crossed the living room to stand near the Christmas tree and touched a seashell ornament. A hollow feeling settled in his chest as he stroked his fingers over it. Sarah had made the ornament for him as a gift.

A sickeningly sweet odor filled his nostrils. He studied Sarah shrugging out of her coat. "Are you wearing perfume?"

"I only wear it to cloak my scent and haven't since I've been here."

"Odd," he mused. "I smell citrus. But I never eat fruit and the gremlins detest anything healthy."

Sarah went preternaturally still. "Oh, crap, why didn't I see it before? Those defenses you set, the safe-guards, they were against anything coming onto your property unless it was invited in, right?"

"Of course. Why?"

She lifted a trembling hand to the tree. "Because you invited them in, Adrian. They've been hiding in the Christmas tree the gremlins brought into the house. That's how they got inside past your safeguards."

He swore softly, and went to her when a swarm of insects flew out of the pine branches, flooding the room in a dark cloud. Adrian's protective instincts flared. He threw Sarah to the ground, covering her as the mosqui-toes flew at them.

They were trapped.

Chapter 7

The whine of thousands of mosquitoes rang in Sarah's ears. She lay still beneath Adrian's sheltering weight.

"Adrian, don't let them suck your blood or they'll absorb your DNA and can clone themselves into you," she told him.

As he pulled her upright, a wave of enormous power filled the air. The black cloud of mosquitoes buzzed and then hit the protective magick shield he'd erected around each of their bodies.

The cloud divided into two. Half shifted into a pack of snarling wolves. They balefully eyed Adrian, growling as they tested the shield again. The other half remained mosquitoes and flew out the opened window.

Adrian's power filled the room with crackling

heat. "Stay here, don't move from this spot or you'll break the shield's protective boundaries. I'll kill the ones that escaped."

He sped outside. Yellowed fangs dripped saliva as the wolves growled. Sarah caught a familiar scent from the lead wolf. Her heart shattered as the tingling down her spine felt like an electrical shock.

She was here. The Morph that had pursued her for ten long years. Sarah fumbled with the silver bracelet on her wrist. Reddened eyes crazed with bloodlust stared her down. She willed herself to see the Morph as it really was. Evil, twisted, greedy for power. Not the Draicon who had loved her.

From the opened doors, she caught the scent of scorched earth, heard bellows of outrage followed by loud cheers. The Morph clones, shifted into a dozen fire-breathing dragons, were being hit with a spray of water from a garden hose by the gleeful gremlins. As the water extinguished their fire, Adrian destroyed each dragon. Breath caught in her throat as one dragon's jaws clamped around his arm before he could kill it. As the dragon died, she felt a faint connection die, as well. Sarah bit her lip. One of the Morphs that escaped ten years ago was now dead. Only one original remained: the deadliest Morph.

She had to help Adrian. Years ago she'd failed to eliminate her enemy and had abandoned Adrian on the beach. It was time to stand with him and finally do what she couldn't face all these years.

Sarah viciously tugged at the bracelet, wincing at the pain as it scraped her skin, leaving her hand bloodied. The bracelet slid off. Magick flowed into her, closing the flesh gouges in her hand. She stepped outside Adrian's protective shield.

She waved her hands, dispensing of her clothing, and transformed into wolf. Bones lengthened, her face became elongated, fur erupted on her body. Sarah snarled at the enemy, baring strong, white teeth.

The lead Morph raised its head. The wolf's howl sang out in her blood and bones.

Memories surfaced of home and a love she thought would never die. *Sarah, Sarah, remember me?*

She could not move, think or even speak, only stand there in mute remembrance. The Morph's form shimmered as if it shifted again.

Sarah raised her head and returned the wolf song in a long, mournful howl of her own.

Teeth bared, the wolves sprang forward. Once again she'd been a fool. Sarah cursed inwardly and mentally guarded her thoughts as she summoned the courage to defend herself.

Suddenly a microburst of air ruffled the fur on her back. Adrian.

He became a stunning blur of speed, attacking and ripping out Morph hearts. Sarah stared with dulled shame at the dead Morphs as their bodies dissolved into ash on the finely polished grained wood floor.

He'd destroyed them all, and she'd done nothing.

Holes made from the Morph's acid blood dotted Adrian's fine dinner suit. Adrian waved his hands, replacing the ruined suit with jeans and a black T-shirt. A single droplet of sweat trickled down his temple. He whipped around. "I see you removed the bracelet. If you were so damn intent on taking them on yourself, why didn't you attack?"

Adrian dropped to his knees, ran his hands over her luxurious gray fur. He buried his head against her neck. "Dammit, Sarah, they could have killed you."

She shifted back, then waved her hands to clothe herself. Energy drained from her, leaving her cold and shivering. Adrian helped her to her feet.

She stared at the piles of ash. "I couldn't."

"Why? You're not a coward. What is it about these Morphs?"

Her throat closed up. Maybe it was finally time to confide in someone. Finally trust. How could Adrian hurt her any more than she already hurt?

Sarah fled into the kitchen, away from her dead enemies. She was finally safe.

And yet she felt only fresh grief, as if someone had sliced open a wound and let it bleed anew.

Adrian's pulse raced as he followed her. Sarah seemed as frail as fine-spun glass.

A merry tune filled the air as a whistling, soot-covered Snark strolled into the kitchen. "What next, Adrian?"

"There are piles of ash in the living room. Put all of it into containers, Snark," Adrian ordered.

Sarah watched the gremlin leave. "Of course. Morph remains are your trophy, to prove you defeated the enemy. Your ticket back to your clan."

Her breath hitched as if she struggled to contain her emotions. Adrian's heart shattered. He waited for her to let it out.

Sarah stared out the window as she braced her hands on the sink. "You lost your clan for a while, but you can return. Not like us. You don't know what it's like to run and keep running, and survive and just pray you can hang on long enough to bear the cold digging into your bones, the hunger digging into your empty stomach, afraid to shift, afraid of your own damn magick leading a trail for your enemy to track and finally kill you. Never fitting in, never belonging. Living as humans, never able to be one of them. Always outsiders."

She whirled, facing him. Moisture sprang to her beautiful brown eyes, shimmering like diamonds beneath the overhead halogen lights. Her body went rigid as marble. He knew her, her strength and pride, and refusal to succumb to weeping.

"I didn't want you to be hurt, Adrian. I never would have abandoned you if not for…"

Guided by the despair on her face, Adrian went to her. Gently, he cupped her cheeks as he tenderly regarded her.

"What, sweet? Why did you leave? Tell me."

Trust me, his expression urged. With all his heart, he hoped she would open up to him.

Her trembling hands clutched his wrists as if hanging on to a life preserver. "I had to save my mother."

"Why didn't the other males in your pack defend her?"

A sob caught in her throat. "Oh, Adrian," she half laughed, half cried. "Don't you get it? The Morphs we fought that day on the beach *were* my pack. I was too ashamed to tell you exactly who you fought. You had a family loyal to you. They loved you. And mine was filled with hate and greed."

Shocked, he could only stare. "How did this happen?"

Sarah released his wrists. "My parents had discovered that my mother was carrying a boy. Because my father hadn't any children other than my sister and me, he'd appointed my eldest cousin to rule the pack after him. When he found out my mother would give him a son, my father renounced Dave as his heir."

A sinking feeling settled in his chest.

"Dave was furious. After all those years, promised to be pack leader and then denied. My sister, Sandra, was angry, too. She was his oldest child, but wouldn't inherit because she was female. Dave needed more power to take over the pack. The only way for a Draicon to obtain more power is to embrace evil and turn Morph."

Adrian stared in growing horror.

"Dave killed his own father, and it set off a chain reaction in the pack, some killing to turn Morph, others dying trying to defend themselves. My parents, my sister and I went into hiding. I made sure they were safe, and begged for your help to stand down my cousin and the other Morphs who were roaming the beach, looking for us.

"That night we faced them, I knew I'd made a big mistake. I could sense it, feel it because she was family and we were closely connected. I knew what she was thinking and planning. I hadn't hidden my parents to keep them safe. I had placed them with an enemy I didn't want to see, an enemy working with Dave to take over," she whispered.

"Your sister." He rested his hands on her shaking shoulders, gently rubbing them.

"When I left you on the beach, it was because I knew something terrible had happened. Sandra killed my mother, blinded my father and was about to kill him when I arrived… My father screamed at me to kill her. I couldn't. She was my only sister, and I loved her! She attacked me and then ran off. My father and I blended in the human world to hide because Sandra wanted us both dead. My only sister, my flesh and blood, who once loved me."

Her voice died on a shudder. Adrian went still, his heart stuttering in absolute fury and grief for her.

Sarah's mouth wobbled tremulously. She unfastened the metal button of her jeans, then jerked the zipper down, the rasp thundering in the kitchen.

"And this is the price I paid that night, when I couldn't fight her, couldn't see her for what she'd turned into. This is what she did to me."

Adrian didn't dare breathe. He struggled to contain his own emotions, knowing this was a moment he must not interrupt.

Color suffused her entire body now as she shoved the pants down to her ankles and stepped out of them. Sarah wrapped her arms about herself.

"Father and I gave our portion of rationed beef to my mom to keep her and the baby strong. My father and I lacked enough energy to heal properly. So now he's blind and I'm a cripple. No Draicon male wants me. Who would want a lame wolf as a mate?"

Her voice was like the hushed breeze pressing against the kitchen window. Adrian's gaze dropped to her left leg, the leg she instinctively tried to cover with her hand.

Deep, jagged scars zigged and zagged down from the top of her pretty lace panties, past her knee, down to her slender, muscled calf. Her flesh looked as if it had been shredded, the bones shattered and never fully repaired.

Silence draped the air between them. He studied her leg, then looked her in the face. Pride stiffened her stance as she yanked up her pants.

"Even when I shift, I can't run properly. I'm not an asset to a mate, but a liability."

Adrian cupped her chin in one strong hand, forcing her to turn his way. "You are strong, sweet. You are strength, and survival and light in darkness. Any male worth his mettle should be proud to call you a mate."

Her mouth moved with uncertainty as she glanced at him. Lurking in her wide eyes were traces of suspicion and doubt, but a new emotion flickered there, as well.

Hope.

He dared to ignite the flame, make it burn brighter. Heaven knew what a cynical bastard he'd been, only green gremlins for company, but he could at least do this. For her.

Suddenly she meant more than anything else. Sarah in that moment became a beacon, focusing all his concentration. He must make her believe in her own worth, and see what he so plainly saw. Her courage, strength, and tremendous endurance, and the life that pulsed so fiercely within her. Like the brightest star in the heavens, guiding him home.

"I understand now, Sarah. If I had known what was happening to you, trust me, sweet, I would have fought my way through a thousand burning suns, a legion of Morphs, hell, a pit of lava, to reach you and keep you from harm. How I wish I could have spared you…"

His voice trailed off.

"I've been so lonely," she said in a small voice. "But no man will ever look at me the same, no man will want me…"

Adrian pulled her roughly into his arms. "This one does," he said thickly.

He kissed her, pouring all he had into the kiss, fusing their lips together in desperate urgency, as if his mouth could soothe away all past hurts. Heal all she'd hidden inside for so long.

After a long moment, he pulled away. Adrian traced the outline of her kiss-swollen lips. No longer could he hold inside what he'd felt.

"Do you know what it was like to be near you, and yet so far away?" he murmured. "Never to touch you, knowing I can never have you, each agonizing moment thinking you had a mate somewhere who would have everything I wanted so badly, to wake up besides you, spend the years with you…"

"I only wanted you. But it wasn't possible," she whispered.

He ran a thumb along her jaw, marveling at the delicate bones and frailness, knowing the steely strength inside the woman. Sarah's eyes closed as she leaned into his touch.

"I don't have a mate, and every male I've sought as one rejected me. I never really wanted them because I could never forget you, Adrian. I'd gladly damn any opportunity to be with another male, if you wanted me, too, even if it were only for tonight."

Adrian brought her face closer to his.

"I'd rather risk a lifetime of loneliness than never touch you at all. One night would never be enough—hell, an eternity of nights with you would never be enough to satisfy what I feel for you, but I would take it and cherish each second. If I had you just for one night, I could walk into the sun and not regret my life leaving me, because I'd be carrying the memory of your smile in my heart."

She tenderly caressed his cheek. "Then let's have tonight."

Chapter 8

They were naked together, just like in her dreams. Except this dream was real, and she was standing before the full-length mirror in his bedroom. Sarah stared at Adrian's reflection, his muscles rippling with strength.

Behind her, Adrian gently wrapped her in his arms, as if he could shelter her from all past pain. He brushed aside her hair, blew a breath on her neck. He kissed her there, sending a quiver racing down her spine as he ran his tongue down her throat.

His hands slid down her trembling thighs, reached in front and cupped her. Spreading her wet folds open, he drew a finger across her slickness. Sarah threw her head back against his shoulder, moaning.

"Look in the mirror, Sarah. Look at yourself, and see how beautiful you are," he softly told her.

She saw herself, flushed, her body trembling with desire, being loved by a man who could have any woman. He'd chosen her.

As she lay down on the massive bed, Adrian knelt before her. He gently pulled her thighs open and stared at her glistening center. Embarrassment at this vulnerable position faded beneath his worshipping gaze. "You are so beautiful," he murmured.

Then he lowered his mouth between her legs.

She felt the slight scrape of his fangs as his wicked tongue stroked over her center. Each delicious flick made the waves of pleasure grow higher and higher. Her hips pumped upward in nameless instinct, but he held her down. Sarah cried out as she shattered like a million pieces of light.

Adrian's gaze was fierce as he straddled her. He palmed her breasts, his thumbs flicking over her cresting nipples. Each sensation spiraled her higher as he gazed down at her with possessiveness. No man had ever wanted her this much.

Nor had she ever wanted anyone else.

As she slid her arms about his neck, Sarah bent her head to the curve of his shoulder, tasting the saltiness of his skin. She nuzzled her cheek against his shoulder, marking him with her scent. "Make love to me, Adrian, be with me, even if only for tonight."

"I'd be with you forever, Sarah," he whispered.

Her hand slid down his muscled abdomen, feeling him quiver beneath her touch. She slid her fingers through the dark, crisp hairs at his groin to his rigid, long arousal. Slight trepidation filled her. He was huge, and she didn't know if she could take him.

He studied her with such a tender look, she felt nothing but absolute trust.

Nudging her thighs open, he settled his hips between them. The tip of his erection touched her wet core. He pushed forward slowly.

"Look at me, Sarah, when we become one," he commanded.

As she did, he gave a powerful thrust, sinking deep inside her. The pain was sharp and immediate. She gasped and writhed, instinctively recoiling from it. He brushed his mouth against hers.

"Shh," he murmured. "Hold on to me. It will get better."

Sarah clutched his broad shoulders. Adrian's powerful muscles quivered as he held still. He was thick and hard inside her. She savored the feeling of being joined so intimately with him at last.

When she relaxed, he began to move slowly. Pain faded into pleasure, then a deep, intensified need with each stroke. She raised her hips to meet him, demanding more.

"You're mine now, Sarah. Mine," he breathed.

With each commanding thrust, it felt as if he sank into her very soul. He took her, marking her as exclusively his, his cock buried deep inside her, his body melded to hers. As if nothing could ever part them.

Adrian loved it, her tiny, excited cries, the delicious scent of her sex, how her tight, slippery heat surrounded him. Masculine pride filled him as she moaned with pleasure. The tips of her hardened nipples brushed against his damp chest as he slid over her. Pushing himself up on his hands, he watched her face. Wonder filled her darkened gaze as he tutored her in passion. He wanted to claim each succulent inch of her, bond them together in the flesh so she could never forget him after this night.

Wrapping her legs around his pumping buttocks, Sarah raised her hips to meet the rhythm he taught her. The sweet, intense pressure built higher. She arched against him, crying out his name as it burst inside her. Adrian groaned, shuddering, as his own release came. He collapsed atop her, his breathing ragged against her ear as she tenderly caressed him.

When they'd lain awhile, trembling and spent, he touched her face. "Are you all right?"

Sarah nodded in a languid daze.

They had tonight, and with dawn, it would end. She must not think of tomorrow. Adrian pushed up on his elbows to regard her in the gathering moonlight.

The stark hunger on his face made her shiver with anticipation as he ran a thumb over the vein in her throat. "I want you, Sarah. I have to taste you," he murmured.

"If you take my blood, won't your clan banish you for good?" she asked.

"Only if you take mine. My blood is powerful and healing, and it's forbidden for me to share with anyone except another vampire. But if I take your blood, I'll create a bond you can never break."

She tilted her neck to the side. "Do it."

The look in his eyes made her heart turn over. "I will not hurt you, sweet. Just lay back, and try to relax."

A low growl, startling in its possessiveness, rumbled from his deep chest. He brushed aside her hair, held her trembling body against his, murmuring reassurances. She felt the sensual sweep of his warm tongue. A slight, stinging pain followed, a sensation of pressure, then a warm tide of intense pleasure. Each erotic suck sent all her nerves tingling, as if his mouth were pressed between her legs. It was too much.

As the pressure built, her muscles clenched, and she shattered, screaming as another intense orgasm swept through her.

He ran his tongue over the puncture wounds, kissed her as she lay in his arms, her body still spasming.

"Wow," she managed, staring up at his tender, amused expression. "No wonder you use a blood bank. You'd have legions of groupies banging at your door if you did this all the time. Even dignified blue bloods."

Adrian stroked a thumb over her trembling lips. "I like hot, red blood. Yours."

She cupped his face, searching his deep blue eyes. "You took me as your kind does, so I belong to you. Now take me as my kind does. Mate with me."

Passion glowed in his hooded, dark gaze. Sarah rolled over and knelt before him. From behind her, he ran his hands down the backs of her thighs. Then he caressed the inside of her thighs, and put his hand between her legs, rubbing gently. She felt soaked from wanting him, every cell crying out for him to take her.

With one hard, rapid thrust, he entered her. Sarah cried out from pleasured shock. He was bigger, harder than ever. He cupped her hips as he rocked against her, his flesh slapping heavily against hers. His breath rasped out in rapid pants, thundering with hers in the night air.

In this position, her wolf flared to life. It howled and demanded. Adrian thrust harder and faster. She screamed, nearly blacking out as she climaxed, hearing him cry out her name as he followed.

Minutes later, they lay tangled together, sweat cooling on their bodies. Blissful and languid, Sarah snuggled against him. She felt cherished. In the safe cocoon of his bedroom, it didn't matter they were werewolf and vampire.

But her practical side warned that time marched forward. They had the moment. The moment could never be enough for her.

Mirrored in his eyes was a reflection of her own torment. "I can't let you go." Adrian brushed back a strand of hair from her face. "I care about you too much."

It felt like hot knives lacerated her heart. She pressed a kiss into his palm. "I feel the same way and I don't want to go, either, Adrian. What can we do?"

"Let's not think about it now," he murmured.

He quieted her with a kiss, his mouth moving over hers. She ran a finger down his smooth, muscled chest, toyed with a small brown nipple, delighting in his sharp intake of breath.

What would it feel like to remain forever in his arms? But how could his family accept her, the despised Draicon?

Adrian glanced at the clock and muttered a low curse. "My father's arriving tonight, Sarah, in preparation for the ritual. I must get ready."

He gave her a tender kiss. She watched him walk naked to the bathroom, admiring the taut curves of his ass. Sounds of the shower began.

Sarah went to the French doors overlooking the dark, rolling sea. Beneath the silvery moonlight, foaming whitecaps crashed against jagged, unyielding rock. She and Adrian were like that, ocean and rock, smashing against each other in the stern restrictions of their separate worlds. How could they merge, and have a life together without one having to give up all together?

She went to her own room, showered, as well. When she returned to his, Adrian was toweling his long, dark hair. Her gaze met his in the mirror.

"I'd like to formally meet your father," she told him. "And apologize for what I did to you that night on the beach."

Vampires did cast a reflection, contrary to myth. But the tormented look in his eyes made her suddenly wish they did not.

He dropped the towel, braced his palms on the dresser. "It's best you don't, Sarah. Not now. He refuses to associate with Draicon."

Emotion tightened her throat. "Why does your father hate werewolves?" she asked him.

"He doesn't hate your people. He merely wants to preserve the purity of our bloodlines. Marcus has always held to the belief that our clan should never mingle with outsiders. He made that rule long ago for that express purpose. My family is one of the oldest and most noble clans." He sat up, jamming a hair through his thick hair. "The rules must not be broken."

"Then you can't break them by having me in your life," she pointed out in a small voice.

His hard jaw ticced violently. "I'll figure something out, Sarah. In the meantime, you must remain hidden from my family."

Hidden? In the shadows, lurking as before, never accepted? "So you want me to hide again, like I used to when your family came around at your beach house in North Carolina? Where this time, Adrian? Should I run into the closet and douse myself with cologne to mask my scent? Or do you have another hiding place in mind?"

Cold dread gathered in her chest as Adrian's mouth thinned. "This convocation is critical to me, Sarah. I must show my father and my clan I'm worthy of returning as his heir."

Yet in his family's eyes, she would never be worthy. Suddenly she realized she no longer wanted to remain hidden. "I've been in shadow all my life, Adrian, even before I got injured. I was always hovering in the background. That's not a life. If we're to be together, I won't be a secret. All that time we spent together, hiding our friendship from our families, as if you and I were something to be ashamed of. I can't live like that."

His knuckles clenched, he stared at her in the mirror. "I can never be ashamed of you, Sarah. But my family won't understand or accept you and I together. Would your family?"

The truth hurt deeply. "No, they wouldn't," she whispered.

Adrian hung his head. Sarah realized what she must

do. Once she had hurt him, deeply, out of necessity. Now she must do so again.

"I have to leave, Adrian. I need to get my father settled into Terrence's pack, so I might as well do it now." She struggled to keep her voice even. "It's time for me to go."

He lifted his head. For a moment something fierce glittered in his eyes. She rushed on. "It's best if I leave. You know that vampires and Draicon, well, we're like oil and water."

His expression shuttered. "You and I aren't. Sarah, I thought…"

"You thought wrong. I could never be happy with a vampire, anyway." She offered a bored shrug.

The pain in his deep blue eyes felt like a hot razor across her skin.

"Sarah, I meant what I said earlier when I told you how much I care," he said in a low voice.

Tears she seldom shed now clogged her throat. Sarah forced herself to speak past them. "I didn't. I feel nothing for you other than friendship," she lied.

Adrian's expression shifted to ice. She turned away, each step like a lead weight.

Sarah went to her room to pack. It was time to return to her own world, and leave his behind.

Chapter 9

Adrian was about to get everything back. Why did he feel as if his heart was shattering? He dressed for the convocation, his chest aching. He knew why. Sarah.

His father and elders from the clan waited downstairs to begin the ceremony of trust to return him to the fold. In the two days since Sarah's departure, Adrian could not forget the Draicon sealed into his heart.

He wanted Sarah at his side each night, in his bed each morning, wanted to make her happy. Adrian longed to watch her eyes darken with arousal as he pleasured her, listen in loving tenderness as she clung to him and called out his name in passion.

But her needs came before his wants. And that was why he let her go. Back to her people, to forget this stabbing insanity crying out they could make it work. Too much was against them. She belonged with the Draicon.

He must release her forever, turn around and never look back.

Feeling as if someone crushed his heart beneath an uncaring fist, Adrian went downstairs to return to his old life.

A shaft of dying sunlight dappled balsam pine branches lining the pebbled drive.

The scent of pine mingled with tangy brine of the sharp, cold sea. Standing on the walkway, Sarah stared at the blue-gray shingles of Adrian's house. She inhaled the crisp air.

James had arrived and settled into Terrence's pack. They had both been welcomed. Sarah boldly faced them and told them she'd loved a vampire, but to her surprise, they accepted her anyway. Even her father seemed to understand. Cameron apologized profusely, confessing Sarah's scars embarrassed him because she had been tested in battle, unlike him. Yet, for all the welcoming hugs and assurances of affection, Sarah found herself throwing up a mental shield.

The only one who could invade her mind and use her emotions against her was dead. Still, she felt the need for caution.

Returning to Adrian's seemed foolhardy, but she couldn't dismiss the urgent instinct to check on Adrian. Sarah glanced down at the notarized statement in her hand in which she testified that she'd witnessed Adrian defeating the enemy. The lightweight parchment was equally thin as an excuse to visit.

Her finger shook as it depressed the doorbell.

Adrian answered. No, not Adrian. This man had his prodigious height, the same chiseled features and burning blue eyes and air of quiet pride, but no scars were on his left cheek and his hair was silvered at the temples. Like Adrian, his fingers were long, lean, elegant, but one fact separated them. On his right pinkie he wore a gold signet ring with an elaborate crest.

The ring was a symbol of his power. Adrian once told her his father never removed it. Ever.

Behind him, she heard people talking, laughing and glasses clinking. The entire convocation must have arrived for the ceremony. But something felt off kilter. Every Draicon sense alerted her to danger. Hairs on the nape of her neck saluted the air.

"You're Adrian's father," she said, studying him. "I need to give him this. It's my signed statement that I saw him kill the Morphs that escaped him on the beach."

The vampire's piercing gaze focused on her like a laser. "You're the one who asked him to fight on the beach. Sarah, the Draicon. The paper isn't necessary. The Morph ashes are proof enough for tonight's ceremony."

She swallowed hard. "Had I known what would have happened, I'd never have asked him to fight with me, sir."

Sarah looked him in the eye. As an equal, even though this powerful vampire could probably snap her neck like a matchstick.

Something flickered in his gaze.

"Please, I must see Adrian."

Please, let me see him. Please, just one last time.

His fierce look thawed slightly. "He doesn't wish to see you."

"You're assuming…"

"No," the vampire said almost gently. "He looked out the window to see who was at the door. He asked me to answer it."

Her heart lurched at the dismissal. Sarah clenched her fists. "I just want to see him, make sure he's okay."

"He's fine…" Marcus frowned as he glanced around. An insect's incessant whine buzzed in her ears. Scenting danger, Sarah went absolutely still.

"Damn mosquitoes! They've been buzzing around since this morning."

Breath caught in her throat. Her senses cried out a warning.

One Morph wasn't dead, after all.

Marcus flinched and then slapped his arm. "Dammit, missed again," he muttered.

"There are no mosquitoes in Maine in winter," she said, her heart pounding frantically. "Please, I must see Adrian. You're all in danger."

Pity shimmered in his gaze as he stepped back. "You need to leave. Now."

Her fists pummeled the sturdy oak as the door shut in her face. "Adrian, open it. It's me, Sarah. You've got to listen to me! Please." Tears trickled down her face.

The door remained locked against her, while inside she knew what would soon happen.

A low, malicious chuckle echoed in her mind.

Sarah whirled and ran off. She could no longer handle this alone.

It was time to call in reinforcements.

Chapter 10

Darkness covered them as the twenty male Draicon hovered just outside Adrian's mansion. The midnight hour rapidly approached. Alpha leader Terrence turned to her, his expression troubled. "Sarah, are you certain there's something wrong?"

Besides her, her father tilted his head to the air. He cocked his head. "Trust my daughter," he murmured. "I sense it. Something smells off."

The other Draicon looked at James with respect. Of all of them, he had the sharpest sense of smell, another reason why Terrence wanted him in their pack.

Sarah took a deep breath. "The Morph that wanted me dead wants me to suffer first. It's after Adrian. It knows how I'll feel if something happens to him."

The Alpha male nodded, his gaze narrowing. "Call us if you need us."

Emotion overwhelmed her. She was alone no longer, and it felt good.

Hugging the fur collar of her sheepskin jacket, Sarah slipped through the shadows. Silent as her wolf, she crept around to the back French doors opening to the living room, and crouched down to watch.

The vampires entered the living room. Removed of furniture, with large red candles in ornate stands placed about the room and only the Christmas tree brightening the corner, the room looked slightly forbidding.

The twenty red-robed figures, cowls concealing their faces, could have been wraiths. She didn't fear vampires, not even these, but something wasn't right.

Marcus stepped in front of the vampires as they assembled in a line. Sarah's nostrils flared. Head bowed in supplication and wearing his crimson robe, Adrian knelt before his father. A heavy sword in his hand, Marcus gazed down at his only son. The air thickened with malice.

If she interrupted this sacred ceremony now, Adrian would never forgive her. The other vampires might kill her.

Marcus raised the sword in the act of laying it just against Adrian's neck in his gesture of absolute trust for his clan. Sarah's gaze whipped to Marcus's right pinkie.

It was bare.

Dread pooled in her stomach. She drew in a lungful of air, catching the fruity scent and feeling the tingle race down her spine.

The glass shattered with a direct pulse of her powers. Through the broken, wide opening of the doors Sarah burst through. "No!"

The shout was just enough to startle Marcus into pausing. Sarah didn't stop, but barreled forward, pushing Adrian aside to safety.

Sarah's frantic gaze met Adrian's venomous one. He stood, tossed back his cowl, blue eyes icy as glaciers as he towered over her. "Sarah, what the hell?"

She heard the outraged murmurs. The others did not matter. Only Adrian.

"It isn't your father, Adrian, but an imposter out to kill you."

Adrian's brow furrowed as Marcus lowered the sword, glaring at Sarah. "Enough, Adrian. Get rid of this intruder before I dispatch her myself."

Ignoring all else but the vampire before her, Sarah raised her pleading gaze to Adrian. "Adrian, please trust me. I'm telling the truth. I can scent it, it's a Morph."

"Ridiculous," one vampire scoffed. "Do you think we would not know our own leader, wolf?"

"Why would a Morph want me dead, Sarah?" Adrian remained motionless, pinning her with his intent gaze.

Sarah's throat closed. "Because it knows if it kills you, I will die inside. And then when it then kills me, my grief will fill it with power it hasn't experienced since the day it killed my mother. It's my sister, Sandra. She knows how much I care about you. I was lying when I said I felt nothing for you other than friendship."

Sarah prayed he would believe her, and take her side once more.

"My son, believe her and you will be banished forever," Marcus warned.

Adrian hesitated and she saw his tormented indecision. Whom to trust? Side with his clan, or once more break with them?

Something flashed deep in his gaze. Adrian calmly regarded the others. "I trust Sarah and I'm taking her side."

Through the ripples of shocked outrage, danger crackled in the air. Marcus snarled. The vampires cried out in alarm as vampire shifted.

The hunched figure with its wispy hair, black, soulless eyes and wet, red mouth hissed at them. The creature shifted, and burst into an explosion of bees, swarming straight at the vampires, then flying upstairs.

Looking severely shaken, the vampires stared at her. Sarah realized they finally understood she was on their side.

"I could use your help," she told them. "You're swifter and more powerful than we are."

Respect filled his gaze as Adrian regarded Sarah. "None of us can scent the Morphs, but Sarah's pack can."

When the shaken vampires nodded, she stepped back and waved her hands, shifting into wolf. Sarah released a blood-curdling howl, calling forth her new pack. Minutes later, they streamed into the house, shifting as they ran.

Adrian took charge. "Each vampire team with a Draicon, find the Morphs and kill them."

He bent down, caressed her fur. "You're with me, sweet. We make the best team of all."

They raced through the house. Sarah immediately

scented Morphs hiding in Adrian's closet. When she flushed them out, they shifted into wolves to attack and Adrian killed them. One by one, the vampires and Draicon hunted the enemy.

When the last Morph had been destroyed, and the other teams combed through each corner to ensure this, she and Adrian went downstairs. Sarah shifted back, clothed herself. "I think we got them all, but I need my father to sweep the downstairs," she mused. "His sense of smell is the strongest."

"I'll get him."

As Adrian raced upstairs, Sarah sank into a chair. Weariness overcame her. Still, she couldn't erase the prickly feeling warning her it wasn't over yet.

Sarah saw a small brown cockroach crawling toward her. A familiar, unwelcome tingling raced down her spine.

Pulse racing, Sarah waved her hands, summoning a steel dagger into her hands.

The roach wriggled, and began to shift. It became someone she once knew so well. Until the day she killed her mother.

"Sarah, I've missed you." Large brown eyes, exactly like hers, gave her a pleading look. "Let's forget all this. I'll leave and you can go on your way. Truce, okay?"

The knife wobbled in Sarah's hand as she stared at her sister, Sandra. Her mirror image.

"Remember all we shared, remember how we loved each other!" Sandra sobbed.

The dagger fell from Sarah's outstretched fingers, clattering onto the floor.

"Sarah!"

The roar of that beloved voice broke through her anguish. Adrian regarded them with a shocked look.

"Hellfire. You're identical twins. No wonder you couldn't face her. It's like facing yourself." Adrian's head whipped back and forth between them. "Sarah, which one are you?"

Sandra's expression shifted into terror. "Adrian, end this before she kills me!"

But the vampire studied her twin. "Do you want me to prove my love by killing her?"

"Yes," Sandra replied eagerly.

"Liar," he said softly. "Sarah would never ask that of me."

Sarah cried out as Adrian lifted his hands to blast her twin. He looked at Sarah, hesitated. Sandra sprang forward, retrieved the dropped dagger and tossed it at him.

"No," Sarah screamed, flinging herself in front of Adrian.

White-hot needles suddenly pierced her chest. Gasping, she looked down at the dagger protruding from her body.

A cruel smile touched her twin's face. Sandra shifted into her true Morph shape and opened her mouth. Finally, Sarah saw her twin for what she truly was. Sandra began to inhale, absorbing her dying energy.

With all her strength, Sarah wrenched the dagger out and raised it in her right hand. Gasping for breath, she stared one last time at her twin, the sister she once loved.

"You're not Sandra. She died on that day."

The dagger went straight into Sandra's heart. Air

blurred as an outraged snarl filled the air. Adrian. Her world going gray, she watched him finish off her twin. As her sister screamed and died, Sarah collapsed.

Chapter 11

Adrian's blood ran cold as he ran to his lover. Blood gushed from the terrible wound in her chest. She must not slip away. He could make her live.

Around him, both vampire and Draicon gathered. Ignoring them, he dropped to his knees. Gently he cradled Sarah in his arms. Feeling her anguish, the agony from the deep wound piercing her heart.

He pressed his lips against her chilled forehead. "Take my blood. It will heal you."

"D-don't," she pleaded. "If…if you do this, your father will forever banish you."

Adrian removed his robe, unbuttoned his shirt. He forced his fingernail to lengthen and made an incision over his heart. His life's blood.

Pressing her mouth against the wound, he urged her to drink. His eyes closed as she finally did. Pleasure at this intimate connection between them warred with frantic desperation. Gently he rocked her as color gradually returned to her pale cheeks. He felt the reassuringly strong pulse beneath his thumb as he stroked her throat.

Trembling, he allowed her to pull away, watching in relief as the wound closed over. The laceration in his own chest healed as he gazed tenderly at her. Nothing mattered at the moment but his beautiful Sarah.

He would pay for this later, but didn't give a damn.

They found Marcus unconscious, gagged and tied with heavy silver chains to the cliffs. The gremlins were nearby, buried to their necks in the sand, gagged and tied with polyester.

After freeing them, Sarah wondered aloud why her sister hadn't merely killed them. Adrian's jaw tightened. "Your sister must have ascertained what you knew, that if they died, I'd instantly sense it. So she left my father to burn in the sun and the gremlins to drown at high tide, while she set about killing me."

Minutes later, as her pack gathered on the patio, Sarah watched in stunned awe as Marcus walked outside, looking fully healed. The vampire clan chief thanked each Draicon. Respect filled his face as he shook her father's hand.

"Once I thought vampires and Draicon could never be friends. I was wrong," Marcus said.

James nodded. "It seems we were both wrong."

At Marcus's request, her pack went into the mansion for refreshments the vampires had prepared for them.

"I don't understand how your twin knew what weakened the gremlins or what I meant to you," Adrian remarked.

Sarah sighed. "We were so close we were psychically bound together. That's how she knew I loved you, Adrian. She felt my emotions and knew my thoughts."

"But how did you know Sandra was masquerading as my father?"

"Your father's ring. You told me he never removed it because it was a symbol of his power. Sandra never knew it because when I remembered it, I had put up a mental block to keep her out."

Marcus gave Adrian a long, thoughtful look. "You broke the rules, again. You gave a werewolf your blood. The consequences of this cannot be ignored."

Adrian hugged her to his side. "I love Sarah," he said quietly. "I don't care that she's a werewolf and I'm a vampire. All I know is I'd rather face the dawn tomorrow than spend another day without her. Even at the expense of losing my clan."

She wrenched out of his grasp. "Adrian, you're his heir."

"That's not as important to me as you are. I will always love my family, but I can't bear the pain of being separated from you again." His fingers trailed over her cheek. "But I'll understand, and let go, if you wish to return to your new pack. I only want you to be happy, Sarah."

Love for him filled her, so much she could see nothing but Adrian. She cupped his solemn face in her hands.

"My father has a pack now, but I never wanted that

for myself. All I ever really wanted was you." She struggled to speak through her tears. "I'd be honored, and happy, to be with you. Even if it means abandonment by everyone else."

"Then I have no choice," Marcus said gravely.

Adrian tensed. But the elder vampire's next words filled her with shocked awe.

"In my foolish pride, I never wanted vampires and werewolves to be allies, for I saw our race as superior. Centuries ago I made rules to protect our people against involvement with the Draicon, desiring to keep us apart and separate from those I considered beneath us."

"You always did live in the eighteenth century, instead of getting with the times, Dad," Adrian said drily.

Marcus looked thoughtful as he threw back his cowl. "Indeed." He glanced at Sarah. "It was a mistake. You saved my son, Sarah, and I am forever grateful. You taught us the value of trusting a Draicon and learning to work with others."

The elder vampire studied Adrian. "I cannot break my own rules, son. But those rules could be changed by a new leader. It's time for our clan to embrace this new century. If you will accept that leadership, Adrian."

Hope filled her heart.

"If I do, you must know I will change the rules, even to the point of taking a Draicon as my mate. If she will have me." Adrian's gaze at her was tender. "If you will have me, Sarah."

Her answer was to slide her arms around his neck and kiss him. When they finally parted, Marcus gave a deep, rich laugh startlingly like his son's.

"I think a Draicon could teach our people much. We would welcome you, Sarah. And I look forward to getting together with your pack, to learn how we can benefit from working together." Marcus clapped Adrian on the shoulder. "Now, if you will, I could use a glass of wine. You have a fine collection of vintages I'd like to sample."

"Open a few bottles, Father. But what about the ceremony of trust?" Adrian asked.

Marcus looked emotional. "You have already proven your trust, my son. To the most important person of all. Her."

Adrian's father went into the house as they stared out at the ocean. Now she understood. The sea crashed against rocky cliffs, but their individual strengths gave the meeting a raw, powerful beauty. Between both existed an unbreakable bond. She and Adrian were the same. Their individual powers made their love even stronger. Theirs would never be a serene, unruffled relationship. Yet she wished for nothing less. Stormy sea meets strong rock in raw power and passion.

Sounds of merriment drifted through the smashed French doors. The gremlins were verbally butchering "Frosty the Snowman" into "Frosty the No Man."

Adrian's hands tightened on her waist. "I know why the gremlins turned you into a doll. We were watching a movie about a man who fell in love with a beautiful mannequin that came to life. They asked if I could ever love an ugly doll." He brushed away a strand of hair from her face. "I told them yes, if the doll were you. Because you would always be beautiful in my eyes, Sarah."

Joy filled her heart. She splayed her hands against his firm chest, feeling the reassuring, strong beat of his heart. "I always thought Christmas was a time of miracles. Now I know it's true. Because I have you, Adrian. I know vampires and Draicon can be friends, and much more."

"Much more," he said softly, and then kissed her.

* * * * *

*Bestselling author Lynne Graham is back
with a fabulous new trilogy!*

PREGNANT BRIDES

Three ordinary girls—naive, but also honest and plucky…

*Three fabulously wealthy, impossibly handsome
and very ruthless men…*

*When opposites attract and passion leads to pregnancy…
it can only mean marriage!*

*Available next month from Harlequin Presents®:
the first installment*

DESERT PRINCE, BRIDE OF INNOCENCE

* * *

'THIS EVENING I'm flying to New York for two weeks,'
Jasim imparted with a casualness that made her heart sink
like a stone. 'That's why I had you brought here. I own this
apartment and you'll be comfortable here while I'm abroad.'

'I can afford my own accommodation although I may not
need it for long. I'll have another job by the time you
get back—'

Jasim released a slightly harsh laugh. 'There's no need for
you to look for another position. How would I ever see you?
Don't you understand what I'm offering you?'

Elinor stood very still. 'No, I must be incredibly thick
because I haven't quite worked out yet what you're offering
me....'

His charismatic smile slashed his lean dark visage.
'Naturally, I want to take care of you....'

HPEX0110A

'No, thanks.' Elinor forced a smile and mentally willed him not to demean her with some sordid proposition. 'The only man who will ever take *care* of me with my agreement will be my husband. I'm willing to wait for you to come back but I'm not willing to be kept by you. I'm a very independent woman and what I give, I give freely.'

Jasim frowned. 'You make it all sound so serious.'

'What happened between us last night left pure chaos in its wake. Right now, I don't know whether I'm on my head or my heels. I'll stay for a while because I have nowhere else to go in the short term. So maybe it's good that you'll be away for a while.'

Jasim pulled out his wallet to extract a card. 'My private number,' he told her, presenting her with it as though it was a precious gift, which indeed it was. Many women would have done just about anything to gain access to that direct hotline to him, but his staff guarded his privacy with scrupulous care.

Before he could close the wallet, his blood ran cold in his veins. How could he have made such a serious oversight? What if he had got her pregnant? He knew that an unplanned pregnancy would engulf his life like an avalanche, crush his freedom and suffocate him. He barely stilled a shudder at the threat of such an outcome and thought how ironic it was that what his older brother had longed and prayed for to secure the line to the throne should strike Jasim as an absolute disaster....

* * *

What will proud Prince Jasim do if Elinor is expecting his royal baby? Perhaps an arranged marriage is the only solution! But will Elinor agree? Find out in DESERT PRINCE, BRIDE OF INNOCENCE by Lynne Graham [#2884], available from Harlequin Presents® in January 2010.

Copyright © 2010 by Lynne Graham

HPEX0110B

HARLEQUIN *Presents*

Bestselling Harlequin Presents author

Lynne Graham

brings you an exciting new miniseries:

PREGNANT BRIDES

Inexperienced and expecting, they're forced to marry

Collect them all:

DESERT PRINCE, BRIDE OF INNOCENCE

January 2010

RUTHLESS MAGNATE, CONVENIENT WIFE

February 2010

GREEK TYCOON, INEXPERIENCED MISTRESS

March 2010

www.eHarlequin.com

HP12884

REQUEST YOUR
FREE BOOKS!

2 FREE NOVELS PLUS 2 FREE GIFTS!

Silhouette®

nocturne™

Dramatic and Sensual Tales of Paranormal Romance.

YES! Please send me 2 FREE Silhouette® Nocturne™ novels and my 2 FREE gifts (gifts are worth about $10). After receiving them, if I don't wish to receive any more books, I can return the shipping statement marked "cancel." If I don't cancel, I will receive 4 brand-new novels every other month and be billed just $4.47 per book in the U.S. or $4.99 per book in Canada. That's a savings of about 15% off the cover price! It's quite a bargain! Shipping and handling is just 25¢ per book*. I understand that accepting the 2 free books and gifts places me under no obligation to buy anything. I can always return a shipment and cancel at any time. Even if I never buy another book from Silhouette, the two free books and gifts are mine to keep forever.

238 SDN ELS4 338 SDN ELXG

Name	(PLEASE PRINT)	
Address		Apt. #
City	State/Prov.	Zip/Postal Code

Signature (if under 18, a parent or guardian must sign)

Mail to the **Silhouette Reader Service:**
IN U.S.A.: P.O. Box 1867, Buffalo, NY 14240-1867
IN CANADA: P.O. Box 609, Fort Erie, Ontario L2A 5X3

Not valid to current subscribers of Silhouette Nocturne books.

Want to try two free books from another line?
Call 1-800-873-8635 or visit www.morefreebooks.com.

* Terms and prices subject to change without notice. Prices do not include applicable taxes. Sales tax applicable in N.Y. Canadian residents will be charged applicable provincial taxes and GST. Offer not valid in Quebec. This offer is limited to one order per household. All orders subject to approval. Credit or debit balances in a customer's account(s) may be offset by any other outstanding balance owed by or to the customer. Please allow 4 to 6 weeks for delivery. Offer available while quantities last.

Your Privacy: Silhouette is committed to protecting your privacy. Our Privacy Policy is available online at www.eHarlequin.com or upon request from the Reader Service. From time to time we make our lists of customers available to reputable third parties who may have a product or service of interest to you. If you would prefer we not share your name and address, please check here. ☐

SN09

New Year, New Man!

For the perfect New Year's punch,
blend the following:

• One woman determined to find her inner vixen
• A notorious—and notoriously hot!—playboy
• A provocative New Year's Eve bash
• An impulsive kiss that leads to a night of
explosive passion!

When the clock hits midnight Claire Daniels
kisses the guy standing closest to her, but
the kiss doesn't end after the bells stop ringing....

Look for

Moonstruck

by *USA TODAY* bestselling author

JULIE KENNER

Available January

red-hot reads

www.eHarlequin.com

HB79518

Silhouette

nocturne™

COMING NEXT MONTH

Available December 29, 2009

#79 LAST OF THE RAVENS • Linda Winstead Jones
Bren Korbinian suspects that his lineage will end
with him—as the last of his kind, a raven shapeshifter, there is only one woman in the world who
is meant for him. Never expecting to find her, he's
stunned when Miranda Lynch visits his mountain and
awakens his desire. But there are those determined
to make sure that Bren is the last...even if it means
eliminating them both.

#80 SENTINELS: WOLF HUNT • Doranna Durgin
Born as a wolf and forced into human shape by the
evil Atrum Core, Jet has only one mission: take down
Sentinel Nick Carter. To save her pack and gain her
freedom, she'll need to destroy the shape-shifting
timber wolf. Which, after discovering their animal
attraction, is easier said than done....

SNCNMBPA1209